Storm Clouds

Books by Lauraine Snelling

RED RIVER OF THE NORTH

An Untamed Land
A New Day Rising
A Land to Call Home

HIGH HURDLES

Olympic Dreams
DJ's Challenge
Setting the Pace
Out of the Blue
Storm Clouds

GOLDEN FILLY SERIES

The Race
Eagle's Wings
Go for the Glory
Kentucky Dreamer
Call for Courage
Shadow Over San Mateo
Out of the Mist
Second Wind
Close Call
The Winner's Circle

9612

Storm Clouds

LAURAINE SNELLING

BETHANY HOUSE PUBLISHERS
MINNEAPOLIS, MINNESOTA 55438

Cover illustration by Paul Casale

Published by Bethany House Publishers
A Ministry of Bethany Fellowship, Inc.
11300 Hampshire Avenue South
Minneapolis, Minnesota 55438

Printed in the United States of America.

Library of Congress Cataloging-in-Publication Data

CIP Data applied for

ISBN 1-55661-509-4 CIP

To Aunty Bobby and my mother,
who read to me when I was little,
thus beginning a lifelong love of words,
reading books, and now writing.

Who ever knows how God
will use our efforts!
Thank you—
small words that convey
a lifetime of gratitude.

LAURAINE SNELLING fell in love with horses by age five and never outgrew it. Her first pony, Polly, deserves a book of her own. Then there was Silver, Kit—who could easily have won the award for being the most ornery horse alive—a filly named Lisa, and an asthmatic registered Quarter Horse called Rowdy, and Cimeron, who belonged to Lauraine's daughter, Marie. It is Cimeron who stars in *Tragedy on the Toutle*, Lauraine's first horse novel. All of the horses were characters, and all have joined the legions of horses who now live only in memory.

While there are no horses in Lauraine's life at the moment, she finds horses to hug in her research, and dreams, like many of you, of owning one or three again. Perhaps a Percheron, a Peruvian Paso, a . . . well, you get the picture.

Lauraine lives in California with husband, Wayne, basset hound Woofer, and cockatiel Bidley. Her two sons are grown and have dogs of their own; Lauraine and Wayne often dogsit for their golden retriever granddogs. Besides writing, reading is one of her favorite pastimes.

1

"MAJOR, I'M SO SORRY you got hurt." DJ Randall leaned her head against her horse's dark neck. The blood bay turned his head to nose her shoulder. "Yeah, I know *you* forgive me. It's forgiving myself for doing stupid things that's hard."

Major snorted and pushed his head farther into her ministering fingers, making it easier for her to reach his favorite places. At five feet seven, DJ had no trouble reaching to scratch his ears or his white blaze, but Major had clearly learned that the simpler he made it for his human friends, the more often they obliged him with a rub.

"You're going to spoil that horse rotten." Joe Crowder, DJ's grandfather now that he had married her widowed grandmother, leaned on the aluminum bars separating his horse's stall from Major's. Grandpa Joe, whom DJ had fondly nicknamed GJ, stabled his new cutting-horse-in-training, Rambling Ranger, next to Major, his old friend from the police force.

"Hey, you scared me! I didn't know you were here." DJ straightened up so fast, she clipped Major's muzzle with her shoulder. The horse threw his head back, returning the favor by knocking her across the stall. She grabbed the stall bars with both hands to keep from smashing her face into the wall. DJ glared at Joe, who was trying not to grin. "Thanks for nothing."

"Far as I'm concerned, it was a good show." He reached out to stroke Major's nose. "Hey, big fella, you sure are easy to spook today." Joe had taken his aging Thoroughbred-Morgan horse with him when he retired from the San Francisco Mounted Police Patrol. Learning how badly DJ wanted a horse, he had offered to let her buy his friend.

"You don't seem too concerned about your granddaughter's health." DJ rubbed her shoulder and made a face at her grandfather. A second look was directed at Major, who was enjoying his nose rub so much that he completely ignored her.

"Hey, you two, remember me?" She planted her fists on slim hips. At fourteen, DJ was stick straight and flat in both front and back, to quote one of her frequent complaints. Her sun-shot honey blond hair waved past her shoulders when it wasn't in a ponytail—which was almost never. This rainy mid-January day, she wore long jeans with both a sweat shirt and a Windbreaker—unusual garb for a girl living in supposedly sunny California.

"You think she'll go away if we ignore her?" Joe asked Major in a stage whisper.

"Fat chance." DJ grinned up at him. "Unless *you* want to teach Andrew to ride. He's supposed to go on the lunge line today, but you know him—he backtracks more than he heads forward."

Andrew, an eight-year-old with a belly-deep fear of horses, was one of DJ's newest students. Slowly but surely, thanks to her patient coaching and Bandit's gentle manner, the shy boy was coming around. She'd led him around the arena on the dapple-gray pony for their last lesson to the cheers of everyone around. That major accomplishment had taken six months.

DJ stroked Major's shoulder and down his injured leg.

Every minute of every day, she wished she had never gone riding up in Briones State Park that terrible afternoon. A mud slide had carried her and her horse over a cliff. It was a miracle they'd survived. Her Gran said it was the grace of God that had protected them, and DJ fully agreed. She'd pleaded for God to send help, and He had. Now they were both well and healthy—well, at least one of them was healthy. Major's leg was taking its own sweet time healing.

She chewed on her lip and shook her head as she felt the heat that persisted in spite of ice packs, massages, and liniment. It had been ten days since she'd ridden him, and it might be ten more. Sighing, DJ rubbed both hands up and down over the swollen muscles of his leg again, feeling him flinch when she went too deep.

"I'm going for the ice boot." She gave Major a pat on the cheek. "Go back to your first love, you big fake." He nuzzled her ponytail before she got away.

"He loves you, too, you know," Joe called after her.

"Right! See if I come back with any carrots for him." DJ trotted down the aisle to the room set aside for the ice machine, the locked medicine cabinet, a sink for washing wraps, and other equipment needed for the health of the horses stabled at the Academy. She scooped out a bucket of ice, grabbed the canvas wrap that covered shoulder to hoof on an injured horse, and headed back to the stalls.

"You riding today?" Amy Yamamoto, petite as DJ was tall and her cohort in hundreds of escapades since they were five, called from her gelding's stall.

"Later. Bridget had an appointment and won't be back as soon as she'd thought." Bridget Sommersby, who owned the stable and riding school, was also DJ's coach, mentor, and encourager. DJ owned a solid case of hero worship for the former Olympic competitor from the French National Equestrian Team, who never accepted excuses or sloppy work from her students. To DJ's unending excitement,

Bridget agreed with her that, a few years down the road, there might be a place on the U.S. Equestrian Team for a girl with big dreams.

DJ marched back to Major's stall, which was housed in the open stalls with corrugated roofing at the west end of the long red barn. Academy boarders could be kept inside the barn, in the outside stalls, or on pasture, depending on how much their owners wanted to spend.

DJ stopped a moment at Patches' stall to palm him a carrot piece. "You put on your willing hat now, you hear? I don't want any surprises." Patches nodded as if he agreed and searched her pocket for more. In truth, Patches would be better known as Trouble. A smart rider never took her mind off the sneaky gelding when riding him. As his trainer, DJ had learned that the hard way.

Back in Major's stall, she wrapped the boot around his leg and Velcroed the straps in place before pouring in the flat ice cubes. As the cold penetrated the boot, Major wrinkled his skin, as if shrugging off flies. "I know it's freezing, but you're tough—you can stand it."

"If that's the worst that ever happens to him, he's home free. Let me tell you, when he took a bullet meant for me and the vet threatened to put him down, I lived in his stall for days." Joe shook his head. "That was a bad time."

DJ stroked the shoulder scar that had never regained its hair covering. She wrapped her arms around her horse's neck and squeezed, and Major sighed as though he liked hugs as much as she did. "You big sweetie, you." She inhaled. "And you smell so good, too."

Life according to DJ meant horses were the best smelling creatures on God's green earth. Unfortunately, her mother did *not* agree.

"You better hustle, kid. I just saw Bridget pull in." Joe ran his rubber currycomb over his brush and banged the two together to clean them. "You want a ride home later?"

He raised his voice because DJ had ducked under the web gate across her stall door and was heading up the aisle.

"Yes, please." DJ dogtrotted to the far corner of the building to Megs' stall. Bridget had ridden the Thoroughbred-Arabian in world-class dressage competitions, retiring the horse two years earlier. DJ felt privileged that Bridget allowed her to ride the well-trained animal, even though dressage was not her idea of fun. It was jumping that made her heart beat faster and her dreams soar.

Lessons on Megs were a sign that Bridget believed in her.

"Okay, girl, let's get you groomed and out there to warm up." DJ took her grooming bucket in the stall with her and, after giving the dark bay mare a carrot, took out her brush and rubber currycomb. Using both hands and the flick of the wrist she'd learned from Bridget years before, she had the horse groomed in record time. She picked the hooves with the same quick motions and had Megs tacked up and walking toward the arena in minutes. On the way past the tack room, DJ snagged her helmet off the rack, then mounted up and trotted across the puddle-pocked parking area to the covered arena.

The outdoor arena looked like a small lake in spite of the tons of sand that had been dumped in the ring. Most of the jumping lessons were held in the outdoor arena, so it was DJ's favorite of the Academy's two arenas. In spite of the landslide, her most favorite place in all the world to ride was still up in the hills of Briones State Park.

She walked the horse one circuit of the covered, lighted arena, then trotted, her posting as natural as breathing. They spent the next twenty minutes at a walk, trot, canter, and reverse, repeating the maneuvers before working large circles and figure eights, half halts and halts, all to limber up both horse and rider.

When Bridget, wearing a yellow rain slicker, opened the

gate and entered the arena, DJ turned Megs and trotted over to stop in front of their trainer.

"You reviewed your last lessons?" Bridget asked after greeting both horse and girl.

"Yup. Working on the bit is so easy on her. Makes me aware how much training Major and I need."

"Good. I am glad you finally agree with me." Bridget stepped back. "Next time you will not argue, right?" Her arched eyebrow said she was teasing. DJ had been as excited about learning dressage basics as she was about math. As a freshman at Acalanese High School, studying algebra never made it to even the bottom of her fun list, while anything to do with horses or art flew to the top.

DJ nodded. "I'll try not to."

"Try?" The eyebrow disappeared under Bridget's Australian hat brim.

DJ flinched. She knew better than to use that word. "I won't argue." Try was not an acceptable answer around Bridget. You either did or did not. You didn't just *try*. All Bridget asked was that her students do their best—at all times.

"Go on now. Review for me."

DJ took Megs through all she'd already done, making sure her transitions from gait to gait were smooth.

"Deeper in the saddle." Bridget called when they cantered past. "Use your seat and legs to drive her into your hands and onto the bit. Shoulders. Elbows. Eyes."

DJ checked each area of her body that Bridget mentioned. Looking straight ahead and sitting perfectly straight with relaxed shoulders, so deep in the saddle that she felt the horse's movements with her seat bones, should have been natural by now. At least that's what DJ told herself. Since she usually leaned forward slightly for jumping, sitting deep and straight took concentration.

She ignored the others using the arena and focused on

both her own body and what Megs was doing. Around and around she went, obeying the commands of her trainer, rejoicing in the round feel of the horse under her. She glanced over at a shout from one of the other riders, and Megs faltered. DJ winced, hoping Bridget had been looking the other way.

Hope wasted. The trainer motioned her over. "Now, what did you do wrong?"

"Broke my concentration and looked off to the side."

"And?"

"And relaxed my seat and legs so I was no longer driving her forward. Megs felt it and slowed."

"Right. Now go again. Same routine."

DJ nodded. When she started to yell at herself, she cut off her words. Bridget stressed positive self-talk—no one was allowed to get on anyone's case, including her own. DJ squeezed Megs into a canter, and the driving power of the horse's hindquarters lifted Megs' head and neck right up into DJ's hands.

By the time the lesson was over, both girl and horse wore drops of sweat in spite of the chilly, damp weather.

"Good. You are improving daily."

"*Merci*." DJ and Amy had started using some French phrases to get ready to take French classes at school next year.

Bridget smiled up at her. "You have Andrew on the lunge next?"

"Hope so. With him off for two weeks, you never know." DJ patted Megs' shoulder. "Thank you for letting me take lessons on her."

"*De rien*. You are welcome."

Back in the arena half an hour later, with an extremely

reluctant rider on Bandit, DJ prayed nothing would happen to spook the pony and scare the boy. His lower lip already stuck out about as far as the end of his nose. With Andrew, the fear wasn't pretend. She admired him for working hard to overcome it so he could someday ride with his family.

"Okay, Andrew, how does the horse feel beneath you?" She kept her voice gentle and a soft smile on her face.

"Big."

"But you remember your last ride, don't you? How great you did?"

He nodded, still not picking up the reins. When his head moved, his helmet slid forward.

Resisting the urge to help him, DJ said, "You better tighten your helmet so you can see where you're going."

He shot her a questioning look, but at her encouraging nod, he let go of the mane and lifted his hands to tighten the web straps.

DJ stood poised to grab him if he started to slip but felt a glow of pride when she watched his heels go down in the stirrups. "Good going, Tiger. I'm proud of you."

He picked up the knotted reins. "Ready."

"Okay, we'll walk around once with me leading, and then I'll let out the line, a bit at a time. Gather your reins." He did. "Good. Now, how will you make Bandit go forward?"

"Squeeze my legs."

"Good."

"And to stop him?"

"Pull on the reins gently and say whoa."

"Very good. And what else?"

"Sit straight, keep my heels down and elbows in, and look between his ears toward where we are going."

"You have a good memory. You sound just like a parrot."

He looked at her, a smile tugging at his mouth.

"You ready?" He nodded. "Okay, tell Bandit to move forward."

As soon as the pony moved, DJ did, too. She kept one eye on Andrew and watched Bandit, the ring, and the other riders. All of them gave the boy plenty of space.

"Good going." At the end of the circuit, she patted the pony and cheered Andrew on. "Just keep doing the same thing and we'll move to the center of the ring, out of everyone's way."

By the end of the lesson, Andrew had exchanged "the lip" for a wide smile. He patted Bandit's gray neck.

"You did good, Tiger." DJ led him back to the stall. "Now let's see you untack him and brush him down."

"You did good, too, kiddo," Joe said after DJ had joined him in the green Ford Explorer. The warmth from the heater felt good.

"Thanks. I never know what's gonna happen with him. But at least we didn't go backward."

When Amy jumped in the backseat, Joe drove the two girls home.

Since she had stayed longer at the Academy than usual, DJ hoped her mother had to work late. That way she could still get her chores done and dinner started like she was supposed to. The closer they got to her house, the more she dug at the cuticle on her right thumb with the next finger. She should have cleaned her room, dusted the downstairs, emptied the dishwasher, and loaded the dirty breakfast things, but she had ignored the mess in her rush to get to Major. *Please, God, don't let Mom be home. I promise to do that stuff first off tomorrow.*

No such luck. Light beamed from the windows of the two-story house. DJ groaned—she was in for it now.

2

"OH GOOD, ROBERT'S HERE!" DJ felt the weight lift.

"You didn't do your chores before heading to the barns, did you?"

DJ shook her head. "You think I'll ever learn?" She leaned across the console and kissed her grandfather's cheek. "Now, don't you need to come in and save your favorite granddaughter's hide?"

"Try to, you mean." Joe gave her a one-arm hug. "Tomorrow, kid, you will do your home chores first. I'll take care of the Major fella. You get grounded, and you won't be fit to live with." He patted her shoulder. "Tell that son of mine hi for me and that he could come by and see his old father since the house he's working on is only three steps from mine."

"Thanks. I will." She slammed the door behind her and headed for the front door. Joe's son Robert Crowder had fallen in love with her mother. Now there was a wedding planned for Valentine's Day, which was also Gran's birthday. DJ had yet to figure out something special for that.

In the meantime, she was about to become the big sister to a set of five-year-old twins, Bobby and Billy, better known as the Double Bs. At times, though, she called the energetic pair things like tornadoes or motormouths instead. Quiet was not a word in either of their vocabularies.

Robert owned a construction company and had purchased a house near the one Joe and Gran bought. Now he was remodeling the house to bring it up to size for his family, which was scheduled to nearly double overnight. Three weeks and five days until the wedding—but then, who was counting? Robert had apologized that the house wouldn't be done in time for the wedding, thanks to bad weather and the snail-minded city planners who awarded permits for building or remodeling houses. Soon after, though, he had promised.

DJ opened the front door quietly in the hopes she could sneak upstairs and change her clothes before meeting up with her meticulous mother. Lindy Randall dressed like a person well on the road to success. She worked hard at her job of selling equipment to law-enforcement agencies and, in her spare time, was studying to earn a master's degree in business. While she didn't *hate* horses, she also didn't understand DJ's love of "the huge, smelly beasts"—her mother's words.

Gran said DJ's passion for horses came from her biological father, the man DJ had met for the first time in her life just before Christmas.

"DJ's here!" The dual shriek killed any hope of sneaking away to change. Robert had brought the Double Bs along.

DJ braced herself. Two matching towheads with identical grins threw themselves at her legs and squeezed hard. Gazing up at her with adoring, round blue eyes, they giggled and said at the same time—a trick they did so well—"We was missing you."

The one on the right, probably Bobby, though DJ still couldn't tell the boys apart, added, "How come you came home so late?"

DJ groaned. "I'm not late, I . . ."

"She's late." Lindy's voice held the flat tone that said she would be polite—for now. That she was speaking from the kitchen did nothing to hide the fact that DJ was in for it as soon as their guests left. The sound of stainless-steel pans clattering against each other underlined her mother's frustration.

"Let's just order in Chinese or pizza." Robert's voice also came from the kitchen. Leave it to him to work to calm her mother down with an easy dinner solution.

DJ hugged each of the boys, trying to ignore what was happening in the other room. "How you guys doing?" she whispered.

"We's good," they whispered back.

"I gotta go change. I'll be right back." She disengaged their grips and headed up the stairs. No matter if Robert helped her mother relax now or not, later tonight would be miserable for DJ. She dumped her muddy jeans in the hamper, frustrated with herself for messing up again. Why couldn't her mother understand how worried she was about Major? It wasn't as if she skipped out every day. Most of the time, or rather mostly lately, DJ did her chores first, even getting up early sometimes to get some things finished before school.

Life hadn't been the same since Gran married Joe and moved out. It was a lot more difficult.

"Get your coat, DJ, we're eating out." Robert met her at the bottom of the stairs. He had a twin by each hand, their jackets already on. "Climb in the car, fellas." As they darted out the door, he took Lindy's coat from its hanger. "Come on, honey, this is better all around anyway. You didn't expect company tonight." He held the coat for Lindy and dropped a kiss on her hair when she put her arms in the sleeves.

"I know, but I should be able to whip something up for supper. Gran always could."

DJ ducked out the door. Robert and her mom wore that sappy look again that seemed to attack those in love. Even Gran had worn that silly look before she and Joe were married—still did. The pause before the two adults joined the three kids in the car told DJ there'd been some kissing going on, too. The melting look Lindy gave Robert when he helped her into the front seat confirmed it.

Sure would be nice if she stays this way, DJ thought. *Melting is better than mad any day.*

Robert got ready to leave soon after they returned from dinner, saying he had to get the boys to bed so they would be wide awake for kindergarten in the morning. He gave DJ a hug. "How are the portraits for the academy folks coming?" he asked.

"Slow. But I have to get busy on them. Mrs. Johnson wants the one of Patches for her husband's birthday." Ever since she'd penciled a portrait of Tony Andrada's horse for his Christmas present at the academy Christmas party, she'd had commissions from other families. Next to riding horses, she loved drawing horses best.

"You guys be good now." She scooped each boy up in turn and, after rubbing noses with them, which always made them laugh helplessly, gave them a hug and a tickle before setting them back down.

"Are you our big sister now?" one asked hopefully.

"Soon. 'Bye, guys." While her mother walked Robert and sons out to the car, DJ took the stairs three at a time. She could hear her homework calling her.

"Thank you, Father, that Mom didn't yell at me," she said later in her prayers. Her mother had wished her goodnight and floated on to her own bedroom. "Please heal Major faster, and help me get all the stuff done that I have to do." She blessed her family, which took much longer than it used to since Robert also had a brother and sister with families of their own. All of them planned to come to the wedding. The wedding!

"We're having a meeting at Gran's tonight," Lindy's voice said on the answering machine when DJ pushed the play button the next afternoon. "She'll make dinner, so don't start the spaghetti."

"Good deal." DJ pushed erase and listened to the next message.

"This message is for DJ." She recognized the voice of Brad Atwood, her father, immediately. "I was wondering if, since you don't have school on Friday, you might want to come up to the ranch for the weekend. Jackie says she'd love to give you a couple of lessons on Lord Byron, if you'd like. She's getting ready for a show in a couple of weeks—maybe you could go along with us. Give me a call." She didn't need to write down the number. She hit erase and dialed her mother's number at work.

"DJ, I can't talk right now," Lindy said when she came on the phone. "Can't this wait until I get home?"

"I guess, but Brad called and asked if I wanted to go up there for the weekend." She heard her mother's sigh. "Please, Mom, I would like to."

"We'll talk about it when I get home."

"But we're going to Gran's."

"DJ, I have to go. 'Bye." The phone clicked almost before the final word.

DJ thunked the receiver down and stomped up the stairs. Up one minute, down the next. Her life felt like a roller coaster, and the hills were getting steeper. Why couldn't her mom just say yes? It wasn't as if DJ went up there every weekend. In fact, she'd only been there once. Visions of the white-fenced horse ranch up by Santa Rosa floated through her mind as she changed clothes. Purebred Arabians grazed the green fields, and there were several mares due to foal sometime soon. Riding Lord Byron, Jacquelyn Atwood's Hanovarian gelding, would be awesome.

She rushed through her chores, finishing just as a car horn honked in the drive. Holding her slicker over her head, she dashed out the door.

"You got your chores done?" Joe asked as DJ settled into the car. With the rain still falling in sheets, DJ's and Amy's bikes, their normal mode of travel, remained stowed in the garage.

"Yup." DJ slid her arms into her yellow slicker. "I'm sick of the rain, how about you?"

"Yup."

"Guess who called? Brad! He wants me to come up there this weekend." She continued without waiting for an answer. "Cool, huh?"

"You going?"

"I don't know. Mom said we'd discuss it when she gets home. You know how she is." DJ clamped her arms over her chest.

"You want to go?"

"Yeah, I do." She told him the entire conversation.

"With all the rain we've been having, he'd better hope the levees hold."

"Don't say that to my mom, okay? She'll never let me go if she starts to worry about flooding."

Joe nodded as he braked to a stop for Amy. "All the rivers are rising again north of here. Some of my police buddies are talking about volunteering to fill and set sandbags—if it comes to that. Pastor said some of the people at church are thinking along the same lines," he added as Amy opened the car door.

"I'd go help," DJ offered.

"Go help what?" Amy shook her head, splattering droplets on DJ.

"Fill sandbags if the rivers flood again."

"They'd never let us out of school for something like that."

"We could help on the weekends." DJ looked over at her friend. "You know, if you don't want to go, no one is twisting your arm."

Amy gave her a raised-eyebrow look. "What's with you?"

DJ shook her head. "Nothing."

"I know what it is. You want to get away from all these pre-wedding jitters that are going around." Joe nudged her arm with his elbow. "I take it you aren't looking forward to the meeting tonight?"

DJ mumbled something under her breath.

"Speak up, the rain is making so much noise, I can't hear you." Joe cupped one hand around his ear and leaned closer.

"I said I wish they'd run off to Reno—elope or something. I hate weddings."

"You seemed to have a good time at mine."

"You weren't all over everyone around you, though. My mother—"

"Your mother has every right to be uptight, and besides, you ask any of the guys at work and they can tell you how *I* was before my wedding." Joe shook his head. "Maybe I *should* tell Robert to elope."

"Yeah. I could go visit Brad while they're gone."

But later that night at Gran's, when DJ brought up the message from Brad, Lindy shook her head. "I just can't think of that right now. Let's get these wedding plans finalized, then discuss it."

DJ swallowed, glad her mother couldn't read her mind. She slowly took her place at the table with the others. When would it ever be her turn? If it hadn't been for Gran's good fried-chicken dinner, she'd have been tempted to walk home, in spite of the rain.

Later that evening, when Joe teased Robert and Lindy about marrying the easy way and eloping, Gran rolled her eyes, Lindy nodded, and Robert said "no way." He said he wanted all of his family around to help them celebrate.

Figures, DJ muttered to herself. The least they could do is get this meeting over with in a hurry—she had homework to do.

"So let's see how we're coming on this wedding." Gran flipped through the pages of a yellow legal tablet and picked up a pen. Since Lindy had so little free time between work and her thesis, she'd asked all of them to help with the planning. Gran read the first item on the list. "Wedding dress."

"Done," replied Lindy. "They said it would be ready next week, plenty early. Oh, DJ, how about if I pick you up after school tomorrow so you can come with me to be measured for your dress? That way all of the dresses will be ready at about the same time. I don't want any of us to cut it close."

"I teach my beginners' riding class tomorrow after school." DJ looked up from the horse she was doodling on the tablet in front of her.

"Is there any time you *can* go?" The sarcasm rippled across the table.

DJ set down her pencil. "After five, I guess, unless you want me to leave school early."

"Sure, and go for a dress fitting smelling like a horse."

Robert gently laid his hand on Lindy's shoulder. "How about if I pick up DJ and meet you over there?"

DJ answered him with a shrug. "Fine with me. Then I can change before I go."

Lindy nodded. "All right. But we should have gotten you shoes before now so we could get them dyed to match the dress. There might not be time."

"If we can't, they won't show much under a long dress anyway." Gran ran the fingers of her right hand through her still mostly golden curls. "By the way, I looked for a dress for myself today and had about as much luck as the sun shining tomorrow."

"Wait a minute! Time out!" DJ used the two-handed sports signal. "What's this about a long dress and dyed-to-match shoes? You know I don't wear things like that." DJ kept from shouting only with a supreme effort.

The look on her mother's face turned from puzzled to purple. "DJ, this isn't *your* wedding. I can't believe you'd be so selfish as to . . . to—" Lindy cut off the thought as she shoved her chair back from the table and went to stand by the window overlooking Gran's roses, her back to them.

DJ sank in her chair, guilt smacking her upside the head. *Good going, DJ. You've really messed things up now!*

3

"YOU KNOW, DJ RANDALL, if you'd learn to keep your mouth shut, you'd do a lot better."

The face in the mirror, mouth foamed in toothpaste, grimaced but didn't answer.

DJ waved a blue toothbrush for emphasis. "If you want your mother to do something for you, it'd help if you'd first do what she wants." She shook her head. Not only was there a pin-slim chance of her going to her father's horse ranch for the three-day weekend, she was still booked for a dress-fitting and shoe-buying trip. Who cared if the shoes matched, for crying out loud?

She jabbed her toothbrush at the face in the mirror. "Now what would really look good walking down that aisle would be my jumping boots. I bet no one would notice them under my stupid dress." She snorted, and a gob of toothpaste hit the mirror. Several others decorated the faucet.

She spit and rinsed her mouth. When would she learn to think before spouting off? The hurt look in her mother's eyes still hung before her face. Even when DJ closed her eyes she could see it—only more clearly. Of course she would wear whatever dress her mother picked out for her. After all, Lindy would only get married once.

DJ thumped her fists on the countertop. "When will I get my act together?" She rinsed her toothbrush, then the sink. Glaring once more at the face in the mirror, she dried her hands and headed for bed.

But even after her prayers, sleep wouldn't come. Finally, she threw back the covers and padded down the hall to her mother's bedroom door. "Mom?" DJ tapped softly. If her mother was asleep, waking her wouldn't be too helpful, either.

"Come in." The tone of Lindy's voice pierced DJ to the core.

Her mother stood in front of the window, back to the door. She didn't turn.

"Mom, I'm sorry. Please forgive me for being such a selfish brat. I'll wear anything you want me to—dyed shoes, even a hat and gloves." *Please, Mom, please turn around. Say everything's okay.*

The silence stretched till DJ felt like a rubber band about to snap.

Lindy rubbed her forehead, a sure sign a migraine was brewing.

Lord, please. DJ could think of no other words. *Please help me.*

Lindy turned, her face shadowed since only the small lamp by the bed was on. "Darla Jean, I want this wedding to be really special for everyone. I know I get carried away sometimes, and I forget to communicate, to fill people in. But you have to do what I tell you. I'm your mother."

DJ nodded. "I know." *Please say you forgive me.* She clasped her hands behind her back so she wouldn't pick nervously at her cuticles. "I'm sorry."

Lindy shook her head. "Maybe this wedding, this marriage, really isn't meant to be."

"Oh, Mom! Don't say that. You're in love with Robert—anyone can see that. And he loves you. For Pete's sake, don't quit now." DJ crossed the space separating them. "Not because of me. Please."

Her throat closed.

"It isn't just you. It's me." Lindy tucked a strand of sleek hair behind her ear. She shook her head. "Well, this is my worry, not yours. I have a lot to think about." She straightened her shoulders, and her sigh sounded like it came from the soles of her feet.

DJ shifted from one foot to the other. She still hadn't been forgiven.

"How can I help you? I mean . . ."

Lindy shook her head again, her hair swinging across her cheek. "Just be patient with me." She reached out, and DJ stepped willingly into her mother's arms. As they shared a hug, Lindy whispered, "And, DJ, I forgive you. All these years, we've been more like sisters, with Gran acting as our mother. So forgive me when I forget I'm the parent now, will you?"

DJ swallowed hard, but the lump stuck. "I . . . I will—I mean, I do." She swallowed again and leaned her head on her mother's shoulder. "Gran says we need to learn to pray together."

Where had those words come from? DJ started to pull away, but her mother's arms held firm.

"I'm working on praying myself first. Guess I finally met something too big for me to handle on my own."

DJ wished Gran could hear those words. She'd been praying for her daughter all through the years—and for DJ, too.

The silence between mother and daughter now felt like a warm blanket. DJ took a deep breath, her mother's perfume filling her nose. "You always smell so good." The whisper didn't disturb the blanket a bit.

"Thanks, at least I get the image right. That has always been so important to me." She shook her head. "But I get the feeling that succeeding in business isn't the most important thing in my life now." Lindy stepped back and cupped her hand around DJ's jaw. "You are far more important to me than beating a sales goal or finishing school."

"And Robert?"

"Definitely Robert, too. Along with two busy, funny, loving little boys." She kissed DJ's cheek. "Good night. You get some sleep now."

"Night, Mom." DJ left the room with the warm blanket of love still snuggled securely around her shoulders.

"Your father called again," Lindy said when DJ got home from an evening meeting at the Academy two nights later.

DJ searched her mother's face for the tense lines that usually arrived with such a phone call, but her mother looked relaxed. Was that a smile lurking in her eyes?

"Yeah?" DJ hoped against hope that everything was going to work out.

"He asked if you could spend the weekend up at the ranch . . . and I said yes."

DJ flew across the kitchen and into her mother's arms. "Thank you, thank you, thank you!"

"I take it this is something you'd like to do?" The raised eyebrow meant her mother was teasing—as if DJ hadn't picked up on that already.

"Only this much." DJ spread her arms wide. She turned her head to look at her mother out of the corner of her eye. "But why?"

"Why what?"

"Why are you being so nice about this? I mean, I know you don't really want me to go."

"You remember how agreeable you were last night,

with no smart remarks about the dress or shoes? And when the woman doing the fitting said you'd need to return to try the dress on you didn't even moan. That's why."

DJ nodded. How could she forget, with the still-sore tooth marks on her tongue from keeping her mouth shut? Much against her principles, she admitted, "We did have fun, huh?"

Instead of Robert driving DJ, Gran had picked her up and been there, too. Since Gran was working under another deadline, she didn't have time to sew her own dress, let alone DJ's. The three of them had gone out to dinner at DJ's favorite Italian restaurant, something they hadn't done together for a long time. Her mother had seemed like a new person. Never once did she suggest they needed to hurry home because she had to work on her thesis.

"Brad said he'd be here for you Friday about noon, so you can get your chores done both here and at the barn first. You don't have any lessons to give on Saturday?"

DJ shook her head. "Bridget decided that since so many parents might take advantage of the three-day weekend, we wouldn't have lessons." She had thought to spend extra time with Major, but she knew Joe would take over for her.

"You're sure you don't mind if I go up to Brad's?" DJ cocked her head to one side, studying her mother. Where had the lines on her forehead gone? And the tight jaw?

Lindy shook her head, then halfway shrugged and raised her eyebrows. "Okay, that's a fib. I do mind. I'd rather you stayed home." She took in a deep breath, nodding slightly as she released it. "But Brad *is* your biological father, and as Robert pointed out, the man should have a chance to get to know the neat kid he fathered."

DJ nibbled on her lower lip. "Thanks, Mom." She thought a moment, then decided to add a question that had been bugging her. "You ever sorry you didn't marry him?"

Lindy shook her head again. "We were too young, too

caught up in ourselves. And now," she paused, "now, if he's as different a person as I am from when we were young, we'd never get along. Besides, can you see me helping to run a horse ranch?"

DJ laughed along with her mother. One thing for sure, Lindy Randall was *not* a horsewoman. Other than riding a horse once as a teenager, she preferred to view them from the edge of the arena.

"You might like riding if you tried it."

"That's what Robert says."

"I know. And don't forget that he promised the twins ponies as soon as we move into the new house." DJ clasped her hands around a raised knee, deciding to take advantage of this time while they were actually getting along. "You ever think what it's going to be like, living in that house all together?"

"Living in that house doesn't scare me half as much as all of us in this one, even for a month."

"Who's going to take care of the twins between school and when you get home?"

"Gran and Joe said they would. The boys' nanny will take a vacation until the new house is ready, then move in with us." Lindy leaned forward and patted DJ on the knee. "That will make your life easier, too, you know. She does housework and even cooks."

"I hadn't thought of that." DJ could feel a grin spread from her heart to her face. "I won't have to start dinner." The grin grew bigger. "I can spend more time with Major." She slapped her knees. "Yes!"

"Let's not get carried away."

DJ looked up to catch the teasing light in her mother's eyes, a light she was just getting to know. *If only we could always talk like this*. DJ wrapped her arms around her knees again and rocked back. "It will be super strange to be part of a family with a dad and brothers and all. Better say good-bye to peace and quiet with the Bs around all the time."

Now it was Lindy's turn to clasp her knees. She rested her chin on one knee and looked at DJ from under her eyebrows. "We've got a lot of changes ahead of us." The silence fell softly between the two of them as they sat in the dimness.

"You think we'll be ready for them? The changes, I mean?"

"Well, one thing I learned in my thirty-some years of life: Changes don't wait until you are ready. They just come." Lindy reached out a perfectly manicured hand to tousle DJ's hair. "You better get to bed, love. Morning always comes too soon."

DJ kissed her mother on the cheek and headed for the door. She stopped just before stepping into the hall. "You told Brad I could come?"

Lindy nodded. "He said for you to call him in the morning. Leave a message for me on the machine so I know what's going on."

"I will. Night, Mom."

DJ rushed through brushing her teeth and washing her face. Sure enough, another zit. Would she ever get lucky and find a flawless face smiling back at her? She dug the anti-zit cream out of the medicine cabinet and applied it to the red spot, making a face at the girl in the mirror. The temptation to pop the thing made her fingers itch. She inspected the spot again. Not ready for popping. She could hear her mother's frequent lectures on popping zits as clearly as if she stood right behind her. DJ sighed, spun around, and headed for her bedroom. Studies called, but her bed screamed for attention.

Her final thought floated heavenward. *Please, God, keep it from raining tomorrow*. Friday! Her father would be there at noon to pick her up for the weekend.

While God hadn't answered that prayer in the morning, He had answered another. For the first time since the accident, Major's leg was cool to the touch and free of swelling. "Thank you, Father," DJ murmured over and over as she rubbed liniment into the muscles and tendons. Major nosed her back and nibbled at her jacket.

"I know, I know. You need hugs and loves, but I'm in a hurry this morning. You know I'm not even supposed to be here, don't you? This is Friday, a school day, normally. And I'm going home with Brad for the weekend, so you better be good for Joe, you hear?"

Major snorted and shifted his weight so he leaned into her. "Get over there, you big goof." DJ straightened and brushed back a lock of hair his nosing had released from her ponytail. She dug the last carrot piece from her jacket pocket and presented it to him. "Now, I'm going to tie you in the aisle while I clean up your mess. Don't go messing out there." She tried to sound stern, but she giggled when he whiskered her cheek.

Joe laughed at them both from the next stall. "You two doing a comedy routine?" He leaned on his pitchfork. "I'll clean the stalls later if you need some time to get ready."

"Thanks, GJ, but I'm fine. Thanks for the ride, too—I'd have been soaked riding my bike. Wish Amy had been ready when we stopped."

"I'm sure sleeping in for a change was welcome." Joe stroked Major's nose. "Let me know when you want to head home. Maybe we could do McDonald's for breakfast. Melanie is already hard at her painting."

It was still strange to hear someone call Gran by her given name. At the thought, DJ could see Gran in her old wing chair, open Bible on her lap and cup of steaming tea on the table beside the chair. That had been the sight that greeted DJ on her first trip down the stairs every morning for as far back as she could remember. Some mornings, she still caught herself looking for Gran, wanting the feel of Gran's gentle hand on her hair as DJ knelt beside her knees, leaning her head into Gran's lap.

DJ sighed at the memory. Big-time changes had zapped the Randall house in the last year. And there would only be more!

One of the biggest changes pulled up into the driveway a couple of hours later. Handsome as a movie star and with a voice as smooth as warm caramel, Brad Atwood greeted her when she answered the doorbell.

"Hi, DJ, you about ready?" A smile much like her own lighted his blue eyes and deepened the creases in his cheeks.

"Almost." She motioned him in. "Joe said the rivers are getting high up north. You okay?"

"For now." He shook his head, scattering droplets of rainwater from his sun-lightened hair. "If this keeps up, though, we could be in trouble. Weatherman said we would get a break this afternoon. Even showed a smiling sun on the screen."

DJ reached inside the closet for her slicker. "I hope so. I'll get my duffel, and we can go."

As she headed up the stairs, he called after her. "Why don't you bring your drawing pad? I've got a scene or two up there that will set your fingers to itching."

"Okay." DJ grabbed her portfolio and gave a last glance around her room. Everything in place, the bathroom shiny and kitchen in order to boot. Amazing how quickly she could finish her chores when she had to.

An hour later, as they drove to Santa Rosa, DJ glanced out the rain-streaked window of the Land Rover at the swollen Napa River, which had spread across the lowlands below Highway 29. The area looked suspiciously like an extension of San Francisco Bay. The Petaluma River was also edging dangerously toward the tops of the levees. Rain pounded the windshield, the wipers wapping at high speed.

4

"OH, WHAT A BABY!"

The little filly peeked out at DJ from behind the safety of her mother. The mare's tail acted as a screen for her foal, draping across the tiny dark muzzle and furry ears. Mother stood quietly, leaning into the hands of Brad, who was stroking her cheek.

"She sure is a cutey. And that's her favorite position. I thought you might like to draw it." Brad shifted to stroking the mare's neck. "This old girl was my first mare to foal, back before I had a barn like this and could afford the stallion that sired this baby. I thought last year might be the last foal from her, but she took again. The vet said she's still in good shape, so we may get another."

DJ leaned her chin on her hands on the top of the stall door. "The mare doesn't seem to mind a stranger here."

"No, she's an old hand with humans, but I once saw her drive a coyote out of the field. That critter ran like he had the devil himself breathing fire on the tip of his tail."

The filly snorted and stamped one tiny hoof.

"She thinks she's pretty hot stuff."

"I can tell. She should." DJ held out a hand. The baby took a step back under the protective veil, but extended her nose, nostrils quivering.

"She's a smart one, too. Of course, with her breeding, she should be."

"Have you named her yet?"

"Nope, thought I'd let you do that. I wanted to give her to you, but Jackie says you will need a bigger horse for jumping, probably one with some Thoroughbred blood. Arabians are good jumpers, but they are better known for their endurance."

DJ tried to swallow. Her dry throat ignored her command. "M-m-me?" The stutter barely got past the desert of her mouth.

"Of course, Jackie also reminded me that you'll need an intermediate horse when you've grown beyond Major. We'll have a friend watching for one in a year or two. Jackie was glad to know you're taking dressage lessons, too. Any and all the training you can get will be a help."

DJ finally located her voice. "Ah." *Now that's intelligent. Come on, say what you think!*

Brad turned to look at her. "You all right?"

DJ swallowed again. "I would be if you slowed down some. You can't just go giving horses away. And . . . and . . . Major will be good for a long while and . . ."

"And what?" Brad leaned against the stall, still stroking the mare's neck with one hand. "Darla Jean Randall, I've got news for you. Since I am your father, I can give you something if I want to."

"S-s-something isn't a purebred Arabian filly worth who knows how much and a h-horse for competition jumping and a . . ." She stammered to a close.

The filly stamped her foot again, dragging DJ's attention back to the baby. *What would it be like to have a horse like her for my very own? A baby to raise and train from the very beginning*. A lump formed in the back of her throat and burned behind her eyes.

"Besides, Mom would have a cow."

"She'd do better with a horse." The twinkle in his eyes brought a smile to DJ's lips. "Come on." He threw an arm around her shoulders. "Let's go have lunch. Jackie is waiting for us, and if we don't hurry, she'll claim I've been hogging you. Let's show her just how generous I am."

Cows, horses, hogs—DJ felt like a herd of each of the named animals had run right over her. She thought about the incredible Crosby saddle her father had given her for Christmas. While she'd spent time rubbing saddle soap into it, she had yet to put it on her horse. Not with the yucky weather they'd been having. That saddle she planned to save for the show-ring.

As she and her father matched step for step out to the truck, she put the thought of horses out of her mind and enjoyed the warmth of his arm around her shoulders. If this was what having a father felt like, maybe having two of them wouldn't be so bad after all.

"So what do you think we should name the filly?" Brad asked as he eased the Land Rover toward the driveway up the easy rise to the house. While both house and barns were on a gentle hill, the house crowned the top. The three barns and the covered arena lay halfway down to the flat pastures that spread to the riverbank.

"I don't know. What are her parents' names?"

"Dam is Wishful, out of My Wish. Shenanigans was her sire. Stud is Matadorian. The foal has a two-year-old full brother and a yearling sister. Matadorian and Wishful have great offspring, so I went for a third. The two-year-old was a futurity winner last year, and the yearling's competitors will have to work hard to beat her, too. I'm getting her ready for halter classes this season."

He parked off to the side of the huge house, built of rust and ochre slate from northern California. Camellias in every combination of pink and white bloomed along the house walls, azaleas flaming at their feet. The riot of color was brightened even more by clumps of red and white primroses. It nearly took DJ's breath away.

She and Gran had worked hard to create a lovely summer garden, but their roses looked pale beside this show. "Wow! How beautiful."

"Thanks, it is, isn't it? Jackie loves flowers almost as much as she loves horses." He laughed and shook his head. "Not really, but they are her second love. She takes care of most of the landscaping around here, especially since she cut back on the hours she spends at the clinic. Says she'd rather show horses now than try to straighten out kids who have been given too many things and not enough time and love from their parents."

He held open the heavy front door for her. "Jackie, we made it."

"I'm in the kitchen." The voice floated from the back of the house, along with a tantalizing fragrance.

"She made focaccia bread," Brad said, sniffing, too. "All we have to do is follow our noses. We'll leave your things here, unless you want to put them in your room first."

"Whatever." DJ propped her portfolio next to the duffel bag Brad had set by the wall. "I do need to wash my hands, though."

"In there." Brad pointed to the half bath off the hall to the kitchen.

"Hi, DJ, glad you could come." Jackie greeted her with a hug and a huge smile when DJ entered the gourmet kitchen. Brass pots hung from a rack over the center island stove, and bunches of dried herbs dangled from hooks above the butcher-block work counter beside the stove. Light oak cabinets, some with backlit stained-glass fronts, lined the walls. Beyond the small table set for three, the full wall of glass bayed out to a redwood deck that led in descending steps to a small pond. Pots of blooming pansies mixed with golden daffodils and bright primroses took the gray from the day, in spite of the rain.

"I love this place." DJ stood shaking her head, admiring everything around her.

"Thanks. I hope you're hungry." Jackie opened the oven door and pulled out a pan of flat, herb-topped bread. "I heard you like Italian food, so I made lasagna and foccacia bread. How does that sound?"

"Heavenly." DJ trailed a finger over the marble countertops. "Can I help you?"

"Sure, cut this bread into rectangles about this big"—Jackie spread her fingers about two inches by three inches—"and put some in that basket. Brad, how about pouring the ice water? You want milk, DJ?" While she talked, Jackie removed a ceramic casserole dish from a second oven, its contents topped by slightly browned cheese and meat sauce. "We'll serve from right here," she said, setting it on the hot pads on the table.

"You've done yourself proud, lady. That smells divine." Brad sniffed the air. "Come on, let's eat."

When they were all seated, Brad reached for DJ's and Jackie's hand. "Let's say grace." He bowed his head. "Heavenly Father, thank you for this food that Jackie has so lovingly made for us. Thank you, too, for prompting me to find my daughter—and for all the blessings you give us every day. Amen."

DJ raised her head and took in a deep breath. She felt so welcomed and at home here in this house, with these people, it was almost scary.

By the end of lunch, she felt like she had done almost all the talking, they had asked her so many questions, especially about the Academy. She helped Jackie load the dishwasher and then the three of them headed back to the barns.

"If you look over your shoulder very carefully, you may catch a peek at the sun." Brad dropped his voice to a whisper on the last word. He held a finger to his lips when DJ started to say something and pointed over her shoulder.

"Shhh, don't scare it away," Jackie whispered.

DJ tried swallowing her giggles and coughed instead.

"You did it." Brad shook his head. "See, you scared it. Now we'll have forty days and nights of rain."

"I thought it was forty more days of winter, like with the groundhog."

"Same difference." Brad winked at DJ and shrugged at his wife. "Groundhog, schmoundhog, rain, drain. All parts of winter. And here I thought we might enjoy at least a moment of sunshine."

"Sorry." DJ hoped her face looked suitably apologetic. When Brad shook his head, she fought the giggles again. "You want me to do a sun dance?"

"No thanks. Then we might not see it again for weeks. If a look or a giggle could scare it away, what would a dance do?" He parked by the barn, and they all climbed out.

"Forgive this man I live with," Jackie said to DJ. "Sometimes I think he is certifiably nuts." She waited for Brad to pull open the sliding barn door. "You want to ride Lord Byron first or Herndon, the horse I used before him?"

"We have a jumper we'd like you to try, too." Brad caught up with them.

He reintroduced her to all the horses in the stalls lining the long barn. "Some of the young stock is out on the pasture, since I figured they needed the exercise. While you two go play, I'll put the rest of these guys out on the hot walker. Matadorian and I will join you in the arena later. You can take a turn on him again, too, DJ, if you like."

"So many to choose from, I can't decide." DJ stopped in the middle of the aisle. Dish-faced horses with large, dark eyes and curving ear tips watched them from every stall. Some nickered, some stamped a foot. DJ wanted to hand out carrots to each and every one. Brass nameplates on the varnished wood doors gleamed in the light from long bulbs overhead. "This looks more like a movie set than a real barn. How do you keep it so nice?"

"Hired helpers," Brad answered. "Most of them have worked for us for the last five years or so. Ramone is the head of the barn crew. He helps us with showing and in the breeding barn. Ramone's been working with horses since about the time I was born, so we are really fortunate to have found someone like him. He took today off, but you'll meet him tomorrow."

"I do most of the breaking of the young stock," Jackie offered. "Then Brad takes over the training. When he's out of town, Ramone and I split the work. I spend two to three hours both training and conditioning Lord Byron most days, and my trainer comes twice a week."

"Wow." DJ shook her head. "I had no idea." She turned to Brad. "You travel a lot?"

"Depends on the case."

"He has quite a reputation as a legal attorney. But he tries to schedule his work around the big shows so we can do them together." Jackie paused while Brad walked one of the most persistent nickerers out of her stall. "See how heavy she is? Due to foal within the month. That should be a real good baby, too. By Matadorian again."

"You sell more fillies or colts?"

"Depends on the year. Matadorian's sons are doing real well in the ring, and this year, we will have the first get from Matson, the oldest. We kept him for ourselves, at least for a while."

"How many horses do you have?"

"Thirty-five—no, six with the little filly you get to name." Jackie took her arm. "Come on, let's go saddle up. If the sun does come through, I think we'll ride down to the river when Brad joins us."

If DJ thought riding Megs was a treat, Lord Byron took

her breath away. Even with her limited use of aids, he responded like a dream come true. Following Jackie's instructions, she rode the extended trot that seemed to float above the ground.

"You ride well for someone with so little dressage training." Jackie held the big Hanovarian while DJ dismounted. "I think you must have a good trainer."

"I do. Bridget rode for the French National Team a few years ago, but when she decided to live in the United States, she forfeited her place. She says she'd rather teach now, but I think something happened that she never talks about. At least not with us kids. She's really a great teacher, though. One thing about her, you don't ever try to make excuses or not do your best." DJ gave a mock shudder. "I won't ever make that mistake again."

"I'm glad you have someone like that. Too many people give up when the going gets tough. You have to set your goals and work toward them." Jackie stroked the near-black gelding's arched neck. "This boy here was one of my goals. I wanted a horse with the capacity for Grand Prix levels. He can do it, too—but I'm still learning." She smiled. "Boy, am I learning!"

"He's a dream to ride, that's for sure." DJ adjusted the stirrups back to the shorter length. "Thanks for giving me the privilege."

"I'm just trying to brainwash you to switch from jumping to dressage—at least that's what your father says. Mount up on Herndon here, and I'll give you the lesson I promised. Then you can take him over the jumps in the middle. He loves to jump and doesn't get the chance very often."

"I didn't think you had jumps," DJ said.

"We do, but they were in storage since no one was using them. Brad brought them out for you."

As if in a dream, DJ took the reins Jackie handed her

and led the dark bay gelding forward a couple of steps. She adjusted the stirrup leathers out for her longer legs, mounted, and checked to make sure they fit. Sliding her right leg back, she tightened the girth and tested again. Now comfortable with the fit, she deepened her seat in the saddle, checked all the points Bridget harped on, and signaled a walk. Herndon obeyed as if they'd been riding partners for years.

"Have you worked on bending yet?" Jackie asked when DJ had Herndon sufficiently warmed up.

"Some but not much."

"But you understand what it is?"

DJ nodded. "Keep the horse bent around my inside leg and ask him to come down on the bit. Keeping Megs down on the bit is mostly what I've been working on."

"Good, then this is the next step. You will work a serpentine pattern down the arena, so you'll need to bend each way as you turn. This increases the suppleness of your horse." She positioned DJ's left leg just behind the girth. "Now for turning left, keep this leg here, shorten your left rein, and hold your right leg behind the girth just a bit. Keep your contact with the horse snug." She looked up. "Do you understand?"

"Sure—until I try it."

Jackie smiled. "That's the way it is, all right. Herndon knows what you want, so relax. Let him teach you."

DJ immediately dropped her shoulders.

"Good girl, now go for it. And remember, sit to the trot."

By the third time through the serpentine, DJ was bending to the left consistently.

"Don't drop your inside shoulder," Jackie called. A few more times, and the right came more easily. Back and forth, up and down the arena. She totally lost track of time, finally picking up the pace. Bending at a walk was the most difficult.

"You did terrific work," Jackie said when she called a halt sometime later.

"Thanks." DJ leaned forward and petted the gelding's sweaty neck. "He sure is willing. How could you bear to give him up?"

"Pure ambition." Brad joined them on Matadorian, who snorted when brought to a standstill. "She wants a chance at the top, and poor old Herndon wasn't good enough. Not the athlete Lord Byron is. We got him from a breeder and trainer in the Netherlands. Another year or so of experience, and Jackie and Lord Byron might make it."

"Might?" Jackie raised an eyebrow. "Might?"

"Sorry. They *will* make it to the big time." Brad shot his wife a teasing glance.

"I'd say level four is pretty big time."

"Me too. It certainly took long enough to get there." Jackie brushed Lord Byron's mane to one side. "You want to jump now, or should we take advantage of the momentary sun to ride down to the fields? You can always jump later."

DJ looked longingly at the series of jumps set up in the middle of the ring. But riding outside drew her like a magnet, especially when the weather had given her so few opportunities lately. "Let's go outside."

A mockingbird greeted them and the sun with an aria of joy. Two of the yearlings raced each other across the green pasture, tails flagging in the distinctive Arab way. Brad leaned forward and swung open the gate, Matadorian responding like a well-trained trail-riding horse. He backed on command and, once through, sidestepped so Brad could latch the gate again.

DJ watched appreciatively. While Major allowed her to do the same, Patches absolutely refused to cooperate yet. "Is there a trick to getting a horse to work with a gate like that? The gelding I'm training for the Johnsons would sooner jump the gate than let me open it."

All the way along the field, they discussed horse training and tricks they had learned to get a spirited horse to obey.

"Calling that clown Patches spirited is like saying a lion is a house cat. I think he's pure ornery and out to prove it to anyone who gives him the tiniest chance. You've got to watch him every minute—he gets bored easily."

California oak trees with naked branches lined the river, giving promise of cooling shade in the summer. Every once in a while, a eucalyptus raised gray-leafed branches, its trunk littering the ground with shredded bark. Broken branches scattered about gave mute testimony to the latest windstorm. Just beyond the trees, the Petaluma river flowed high up the diked banks, brown with runoff soil.

The trunk of a willow tree floated downstream, its roots waving sadly to the sky. It caught on a fallen tree from the opposite side of the river and hung there before swirling on down toward the Bay.

"At least the river is falling today. That's good." Brad reined his mount to a stop. "If the storms let up, we'll be okay. The Petaluma doesn't usually get it as bad as the Russian River north of here."

DJ watched the willow tree float away. It was moving pretty fast. A cloud covered the sun, sending shivers up her back. The river looked like a swollen brown snake between the banks of green. She never had liked snakes much.

"You want to jump now?" Jackie asked when Brad rode on ahead. "He'd rather patrol the perimeters of his camp, like a good commander. We'll ride back here again during the summer when we can walk the horses right into the river, just around that bend."

Within minutes, Jackie had the jumps adjusted for DJ's training level. She moved off to watch, Lord Byron's reins looped over her arm.

DJ felt a thrill shoot through her. Jumping again! It felt like she hadn't jumped in months, maybe even years. She set Herndon into a canter and toward the first jump. He lifted off at just the right moment and landed so lightly, she felt like she was still flying. She could hear Jackie's applause and Brad cheering her on as he rejoined them. The second jump, the third, and the fourth—each one renewed the thrill. This was what she lived for, those brief moments when she was airborne. There was no feeling like it anywhere else on earth. At least nothing she had ever felt.

DJ finished the sixth and continued the canter to where Brad and Jackie sat on their horses.

"That was great!" Brad's face shone with his excitement.

Jackie nodded. "You did well. Shall I raise them?"

"Okay, but not much. Bridget says to keep the jumps low enough for a good workout, yet high enough to learn something. What I learned this time is that Herndon loves to jump. You see his ears? Forward the whole time." She patted the horse's neck. "Herndon, old boy, you've got a permanent friend in me."

This round, they ticked on the fifth jump, and the pole came tumbling down. "Rushed that one, fella, and I got left behind. Sorry. Let's go again." She cantered back around to jump one and began the circuit again, this time concentrating on her timing. Bridget always said to count the beats between jumps, and DJ had skipped doing that on the tick round. When DJ finished with a clean slate this time through, Jackie asked if she should raise the poles again.

DJ hesitated. If this were a jump-off like those Hilary had to ride in almost every show, the poles would go higher. Should she do it?

She nodded, and Brad set the fifth jump higher than she had ever jumped.

They cantered forward, Herndon's ears forward, joy in

his every step. They cleared the first four with space to spare. DJ felt like she was part of a flying machine.

"Okay, fella, let's do this one, too."

They cantered toward the jump with three poles, the bottom two in an X-crossed pattern below the top one. DJ leaned forward, but Herndon swerved to the right.

DJ went airborne.

5

DJ COULD FEEL SOMETHING WARM and sticky running down the left side of her face.

"DJ, are you all right?" Brad reached her as she gingerly sat up. "Oh my word—you're bleeding!"

DJ raised a hand to her cheek and came away with blood on her glove. "Other than this scratch, I'm fine, I think." She wiggled her toes, flexed her knees and ankles, and put a hand back on the ground to lever herself up. She looked up into her father's face. If she was as white as he, she must look a sight. Red blood, white skin. *Oh, great. Just great!*

"Thank God for helmets," Jackie said as she knelt by DJ's side. "You must have hit the base of the standard." She reached over her shoulder for the folded handkerchief Brad handed to her. "Let's get this on that cut before you bleed to death." Her smile reassured DJ that bleeding to death wasn't really an option.

If all the heat in her face originated with the cut, that would be fine. But feeling like an idiot usually brought its own hot skin. What a dumb thing to do—let Herndon dump her just because he didn't want to jump the fence. She'd ridden other horses who had refused a jump. You had to be ready, that's all. "Where's Herndon? Is he all right?"

"That fool horse is fine. It's you I'm worried about." Brad knelt at her other side.

"I shoulda been paying better attention. To let him dump me like that . . ." She shook her head.

"DJ, falls happen to the best riders. Hitting the ground goes with the territory." Jackie pressed harder on the pad.

"I know, but . . ." DJ kept herself from flinching away. The cut was beginning to burn.

"No buts." Brad extended a hand to pull her to her feet. "Let's go get that cleaned up and see if you need a couple of stitches."

"Stitches!" DJ could feel her mouth drop open. "I won't need stitches." She looked at Jackie. "Will I?" Her voice squeaked. *The wedding!* Would her face heal in time for the wedding, now only three weeks away? "Mom's going to kill me."

"Why? She should be glad you're not hurt any worse." Brad still wore a white ring around his mouth. "Thank God you aren't hurt any worse. Or are you? Can you walk? How's your shoulder? I should never have raised the jumps that last time. It's all my fault."

"Huh? What's this fault garbage? I took a header, that's all. It wasn't my first, and I'll bet anything it won't be my last."

Jackie smiled up at her husband. "Listen to your daughter, dear. In spite of getting clobbered by Herndon, she has her head on straight." She turned back to DJ. "Come on, let's see if anything else hurts. You'll most likely get a black eye from this, too, since it's right on the cheekbone."

DJ groaned again.

"You hurt somewhere else?" Brad stopped her with a hand on her arm.

"No, but I probably will hurt in all kinds of places

tomorrow. Can you just see a wedding where the bridesmaid has a black eye?"

"Oh no." Now it was Brad's turn to groan. "I forgot all about the wedding." Brad turned from them at the arena gate. "You take her on up to the house, Jackie, and I'll put the horses away."

"I should make Herndon go back and take that fence." DJ started to turn back.

"I don't think so." Brad shook his head. "You some kind of masochist?"

"No, she's just like her father—thinking of the horse before herself." Jackie took DJ's arm, as if to keep her from turning back. "Come on, DJ, let's see what we have here. See you in a few minutes, Brad."

The warmth from the Land Rover's powerful heater felt good since the sky had reverted to gray while they played in the arena. DJ shivered a bit and caught herself before she called herself any names. She could hear Bridget's voice reminding her to let it go. *Don't beat yourself or your horse*. How many times had she heard that bit of wisdom?

"I think we better take you in to the urgent care clinic up in Santa Rosa." Jackie tilted the light in the bathroom so she could see better. "That cut looks deep and long enough that a butterfly bandage might leave you with more of a scar than stitches would."

DJ groaned. "I hate going to doctors. They take forever."

"I know. But your father will feel better about it. So will I." She handed DJ a sterile pad. "Hold this in place while I get some ice. Let's get that swelling down, if we can." When she returned with ice in a zipped plastic bag, DJ applied that to the pad.

"I'm going to call the clinic and tell them we're coming."

"How long since you've had a tetanus shot?" the doctor asked as he examined the cut.

DJ shrugged. "I don't know. Can't remember when."

"Why don't you call her mother and ask?" the doctor said to Jackie.

"Can't you just give me one? My mom gets kinda uptight about stuff like this."

"It's better to check." He turned and gave instructions to the nurse.

As Jackie started to leave, DJ said, "Call Gran instead. She's the one who kept track of stuff like this. And please ask her not to tell Mom. Beg if you have to. Telling Mom now would ruin everything."

"I'll try." Jackie wiggled her fingers as she went out the door.

"You want to tough this out, or would you rather have a bit of Novocain?" The doctor looked at her over the tops of his half glasses.

"How bad will the stitches hurt?" While she didn't mind giving shots to a horse, needles puncturing her own hide had never been a real favorite of hers. Not even close.

"I think the shot hurts as bad as the stitches, but that's only my opinion."

"No shot then," DJ said, eyeing the needle. The last time she'd had stitches was when she'd fallen out of a tree, years ago now. She'd ripped her knee on the branch that had cracked on the way down, but at least she hadn't broken any bones. Gran always said DJ had fallen on a guardian angel. She even claimed she'd heard an extra *oof* when DJ hit the ground.

"Ready?" The doctor smiled at her.

DJ nodded. This time she wouldn't be able to watch.

She told herself to relax when she lay against the pillow. She felt the nurse's hands cupping her head to keep her from jerking away.

Jackie reentered the room just before the doctor began. "Her grandmother says it's been five years since her last tetanus shot. And, DJ, she promised to let you do the talking when you get home."

DJ started to nod, then stopped. "Good."

Within minutes, she was stitched, bandaged, inoculated, and walking out the door. Brad leaped to his feet in the waiting room. "You okay?" At DJ's nod, he turned to Jackie. "They stitched it?"

"Yes, worrying father, and your daughter is a trooper. Stitches without Novocain even."

"Stitches, as in with a needle?" At DJ's nod, he continued. "And you didn't faint?"

"Faint?" She changed from a grin to a straight face when the bandage crinkled. "Ouch."

"Don't mind your father. He faints when a needle gets near him."

"Not quite. Only when it pokes me. I just get dizzy before that." He reached a gentle hand to touch the bandage. "I'm so sorry, DJ."

DJ rolled her eyes and made Jackie laugh. Rather, she rolled one eye. The left one was now swollen halfway shut.

Once in the Land Rover, DJ leaned back and put the ice pack back on her face.

"The seat tilts," Jackie said. "And remember, the doctor gave you some pain pills in case it starts hurting too badly. You don't need to tough it out—the body heals faster when it isn't fighting pain, too."

"It hurts, but let's try some Tylenol first. I hate that fuzzy feeling from pain-killers."

They stopped at a convenience store and bought her a bottle of water to take the Tylenol with, so by the time they got back to the ranch, DJ was feeling pretty good again. But when she suggested she would like to go back to the arena and make Herndon take the jump, Brad looked at her as if she'd cracked her mind in the fall.

"I don't *think* so." He looked to Jackie as if for support. She just shrugged. "Maybe you better lay down for a while."

DJ returned his cracked-mind look. She knew how to raise her eyebrows in just the same way he did, but she'd never dreamed that it was a trait she'd gotten from her father.

"Okay, how about coming with me to check on the mares? You could try out some names for the baby."

DJ turned to Jackie. "I could help you with dinner if you like."

"Thanks, sweetie, but I already made soup. You go with your dad and have a good time."

It was the first time in her life someone had called her "sweetie," but DJ didn't mind a bit. From Jackie, it sounded just right. She followed her dad out to the truck, trying to duck between the raindrops since she had left her slicker down at the barn. "Do you always drive back and forth?" she asked when he had the truck in motion.

"Pretty much. Unless it's really a nice day and I'm not in a hurry. Those days come few and far between, I'm afraid."

"What is your work like?" She turned so she could see him better out of her one good eye.

"Not like what you see on television or the movies. Most legal work involves tons of reading, writing, and talking on the phone with clients. Since I'm not a trial attorney, I don't spend a lot of time in court. I have some really sharp associates for that end of the business. They like the spotlight, and I like having a life besides the law." He motioned to the farm around them. "If I could, I'd retire tomorrow and go full time into horse breeding."

"You can't?"

"Nope, I keep my practice going to support my horse habit. Since the bottom fell out of Arabian breeding, it's hard to get ahead. Plus, we like to show, and Jackie is serious about wanting to compete on the Grand Prix level. International shows take a lot of time and money."

"Local shows are bad enough." DJ leaned back against the seat. "Mom always said having a horse was too much for our budget. Thing is, she's right. If I didn't work for Major's board and then some, I couldn't keep him."

"DJ, are you short on money?"

"No. Why?" She thought back to what she'd said. "Oh no, don't get the wrong idea. I didn't mean—I mean—" She took a deep breath and sighed. "I like working at the Academy, even mucking stalls when I have to. I like training Patches and will take on another when he is ready to leave me. Sure, vet bills are spendy and shoeing costs more than I'd like, but that's part of owning a horse. Major is my responsibility."

"And you're a responsible person?"

"Yeah, I am."

"I can tell. You make me so proud I could pop." He clasped his hands along the top of the steering wheel and turned his head to look at her. "Take today, for example—the way you handled the fall and getting stitched up—not to mention your riding ability, the wonderful way you draw, your sense of humor." He gave her a smile that showed his feelings of pride and love. "Your mother has done a fine job with you."

"Gran did most of the work." DJ immediately wished she'd kept her mouth shut. The comment bordered on being less than nice.

"Well, then I can thank Melanie, too. She always was a woman of wisdom."

DJ picked at a cuticle. When her courage grew strong enough, she said, "Can I ask you a question? One that's been eating at me?"

He nodded. "Ask away, and I'll answer if I can."

DJ kept her gaze on his face. "Why did you never write or call me?"

Silence swelled in the truck cab, the rain on the roof sounding like a drum roll.

DJ wished she had kept her mouth shut.

Brad nodded slightly. "I could give you all kinds of reasons, most of them valid, but the bottom line is I was chicken. I had bowed out of your life, and I was afraid Lindy hated me and had made you hate me, too."

"Mom never said a word about you—ever. Once or twice I wondered, but since I was happy, I figured I didn't need a dad—not when I had Gran and Gramps and Mom. Even after Gramps died . . . our little family felt like enough. I sure missed Gramps, though—for a long time." DJ spoke slowly and softly, exploring the ideas herself as she shared them with her father.

"I missed out on a lot."

"Gran says everything happens in God's timing."

"Yes, I'm sure she does. Melanie always did have a strong faith. She's an example to all of us. No way I'd hear such talk from my family."

"But you believe now?"

"Thanks to Jackie. Still, I might never have contacted you if we had been able to have children. Maybe this is God's way, after all." He reached out and stroked a gentle finger down the curve of her cheek. "I am just so eternally grateful that I know you now. 'If onlys' aren't worth the time it takes to think about them." He patted her hand. "Any more questions?"

"One more?"

"Shoot."

"What do I call you? Before long, I'm going to have two dads or whatever, and I don't know what to call either one of you."

"Let me think on that one, okay? Who knows, maybe you'll come up with something that you feel comfortable with on your own. Eventually, something will work out. Just please don't ever introduce me as Mr. Atwood."

"I won't."

"And, DJ, if Lindy and Robert can handle it, I really want to be a part of your life. Jackie and I both do."

"Things like school and stuff, too?"

"Yep. All of it. Shows, school events, birthdays. Whatever."

"Cool."

Together they walked into the barn and over to the only foaling stall in use at the moment. The filly darted behind her mother and peeked out just like before as the mare hung her head over the low wall to soak up the attention. When Brad obliged by scratching up behind her ears and down her cheek and neck, the mare sighed and let her eyelids close. When he stopped, she tilted her head to coax him to keep going.

DJ leaned over the gate, extending her hand to the filly.

The curious baby reached out her muzzle and leaned toward the hand. But she refused to move a foot closer.

"You should call her Elusive. Ellie for short."

"That's a great name. And it sure fits her temperament—at least what we've seen of it so far. If you want to go inside the stall and just sit in the corner, this old girl won't mind. You'll be able to make friends with Ellie there. I'll finish my chores and come back for you."

"You sure my face won't scare her?"

"DJ!" He dug in his pocket and pulled out pieces of horse cookies. "She won't take these yet, but I know her mother loves them."

DJ opened the stall door very slowly and slipped inside. The filly disappeared behind her mother. The mare wandered over and lipped the cookie bits from DJ's palm, then, munching, gave DJ the nose test. Up her arm, her hair, and finally her jacket pockets.

"You found 'em, huh?" DJ gave the mare another treat while scratching her ears. "Why don't you tell your kid to come visit with me, too? You mind if I sit here in the corner?" As she talked, she slid her back down the wall and crossed her legs to sit comfortably. The mare lowered her head and, after sniffing some more to check out the bandage, blew horse-cookie breath in DJ's face.

"Thanks a big fat bunch." DJ wiped away a bit of slobber. While she paid attention to the mare, she kept her eye on the baby, who hid behind her mother's tail again, peeking out from the veil.

"Curiouser and curiouser, aren't you?" At the low, singsong hum of DJ's voice, the baby ears flicked back and forth. One step at a time, she edged around her dam until she was standing clear, a strand of the mare's long tail still caught on one fuzzy ear. DJ kept herself from laughing out loud only through sheer effort of will.

"Such a charmer, you are. How could anyone resist you? How can you keep from coming over here to see what is pleasing your mom so much?" The mare stood, eyes at half-mast, her nose even with DJ's shoulder.

The filly finally stood within a foot of DJ, her body poised to flee at the slightest mismove. DJ kept playing with the mare.

When she worked her arm up to rub behind the mare's ears, the baby reached out and sniffed DJ's sleeve. When nothing happened, she took a step closer. The mare whuffled DJ's hair, and DJ slipped her another treat. Loud munching filled the stall.

DJ could feel her right foot going to sleep. Soon, she

would have to move. "Come on, baby, make it all the way over here. Let me touch you the way I am your mother. I promise you you'll like it."

Ellie sniffed DJ's hair, then darted back one step. She reached again, brushing DJ's hand with the whiskers on her upper lip. At last, she sighed and let DJ touch her nose. Ears pricked, eyes wide, little Miss Elusive huddled closer to her mother's shoulder and let DJ stroke her furry cheek and under her chin.

"What a baby you are . . . so soft." DJ wanted to shout for joy. She'd done it! She'd petted Elusive.

"You really have a way with horses, my dear," Brad spoke softly from above her head.

The filly darted behind her mother again, so DJ pushed herself upright. Needles stabbed her awakening right foot, and she grabbed on to the stall door. "I didn't even hear you come up."

"You were too busy. Such patience that took. No wonder you are able to win even Patches over."

DJ limped out the stall door when Brad swung it open. "Thanks for the treat. What a honey she is."

"Let's go eat, then talk about you drawing her."

Before she left for home Sunday afternoon, DJ had ten drawings scattered over the table. She'd also ridden again, working Herndon until he cleared all the jumps nicely. Another ride on Lord Byron after a dressage lesson on Herndon reminded her again of how much there was ahead to learn.

When DJ called home, Lindy said they would all be over at Gran's, so she should be dropped off there.

"Do you want to come in?" DJ asked when Brad stopped the Land Rover in Gran's driveway.

"Not this time, unless you want me to." He motioned to her face, which at least was no longer swollen.

"Nah, it's no big deal. Thanks for the wonderful weekend. You'll call me when that other mare is about to foal?"

"If it looks like it will happen on a weekend." He squeezed her shoulder. "Take care of yourself, kid."

DJ leaped from the car with all her gear and, after one more wave, trotted to the front door. She had so much to tell everyone!

"Hi, I'm back," she called from the entrance.

The two torpedoes hit her at the same time, but she was braced and ready. She reached down and hugged them, one arm around each. "Hi, guys."

They looked up, their mouths going round as their eyes. "DJ, what did you do?"

She put a finger over her lips to shush them. When she looked up, her mother and Robert stood before her.

"Darla Jean Randall, whatever happened to your face?" Lindy's face matched the shock in her voice.

6

"IT LOOKS WORSE THAN IT IS." DJ put a hand to her bandaged cheek.

Lindy's horrified question brought Gran and Joe to the hallway. When DJ looked at her grandmother, Gran shook her head. No, she hadn't mentioned anything about the accident.

Robert put an arm around Lindy's shoulders. "Okay, DJ, fill us in."

DJ set her things out of the way and joined everyone in the living room. With all eyes on her, she swallowed and related what had happened. "So it's just a couple of stitches. I know I have a black eye, but it's getting better." She blinked both eyes for good measure. "Most of the swelling is gone already."

"So you were jumping with a horse you didn't know?" Lindy leaned forward, away from Robert.

The boys had glued themselves to DJ's side as if assigning themselves as her protectors. Every once in a while, one would moan, "Poor DJ."

By the third "poor DJ," she nearly burst out laughing. But she could tell her mother was in no mood for laughter.

"Come on, Mom, it's no big deal. I'm not broken anywhere. If I never get hurt any worse than this, I'll be blessed." *Oops, not the right thing to say*. The frown deepened between her mother's eyes, and DJ sent Joe a pleading glance.

"She's right, Lindy. She's not seriously hurt, and we'll all keep praying that she never will be." Joe smiled at DJ. "Besides, Gran has been sending guardian angels DJ's way for fourteen years now. I'd say they're doing a pretty good job."

"I just don't want Brad Atwood being irresponsible with my daughter."

DJ bit her tongue.

"No one was irresponsible. Accidents happen." Robert rubbed Lindy's shoulder and drew her back into the circle of his arm. "Remember when Bobby took a header off the bleachers? Was that my fault for not watching him better? Or yours? Or DJ's? Or Dad's? We were all there."

DJ sat back in her chair in relief. "Thanks, Robert."

As the conversation turned to other things, DJ regaled them with the tales of Elusive. She brought out her drawings and made the boys giggle at the baby peeking out from her mother's tail.

"These are about your best yet," Gran said, holding the pencil drawings up for better light. "She sure is a sweetheart."

"Yeah, and I finally got her to come to me." DJ told that story, then went on about the possible flood, the gorgeous yard, riding Lord Byron, taking lessons from Jackie, and what great food they had.

Lindy jerked up a restraining hand. "Enough already. DJ, you're not letting anyone else get a word in edgewise." Her look shouted "be quiet!"

"Oh, sorry." DJ slumped back. She watched her mother for any sign of relenting. She still had so much to tell. Wasn't she interested? The boys leaned against her knees.

"DJ, tell us more stories," one pleaded, the other nodding.

"How about we kids go in the other room and let the grown-ups talk all they want?" She didn't even try to keep the sarcastic bite out of her words. DJ looked up to catch a questioning look from Robert. Gran just shook her head.

Letting the boys pull her to her feet, DJ and her escorts left the room. They settled in the family room, all three in Joe's big recliner. DJ told them again about the filly, this time making it more of a story. "The Adventures of Elusive, Ellie for Short." Whenever she asked, "And do you know what happened then?" the boys gave her another idea, and off the story would go again. Then she drew pictures to illustrate the story and let the boys color them.

By the time they were ready to leave, DJ had pretty much forgotten about her hurt feelings, but when they got home, she knew for certain her mother hadn't.

"I didn't appreciate your sassy remark," Lindy said before DJ went up the stairs. "I also think you should have called me to say you'd had an accident."

"Sorry." DJ knew if she said anything more, another smart remark might explode into the air. Why would she want to call when her mother probably would have ordered her to come home at once?

"Brad at least should have had the courtesy to call."

"But, Mom—"

"No buts." Lindy took another tack. "Is your homework done?"

DJ shook her head. "I forgot to take it with me. It's not Brad's fault."

"Well, someone in this family has to be responsible."

Sorry didn't seem to be cutting it, so DJ chose not to say it again. "Good night, Mother. I'll try to do better." She stomped on the first step of the stairs but changed her footing fast. She would not get into a fight and ruin the entire weekend.

But the old "not fairs" raged in DJ's head, keeping her

from falling asleep. Here she had been so excited about her visit and all the neat things that happened, and her mother got into a hissy fit. All Lindy could think of was homework and who was responsible. Who was her mother to say that? Until the last year, she'd hardly ever asked about homework—and never about the Academy. Gran had done all the asking, just like Gran had done everything around the house. Lindy hadn't done much of anything but work, go to school, come home, and study. She hardly took a minute in her loaded schedule for her daughter.

DJ flipped over on her other side. Let God see if He could figure this one out—she sure couldn't. But the Bible verses she'd memorized in Sunday school started a parade through her wide-awake mind. *Honor your father and your mother, so that you may live long in the land the LORD your God is giving you. . . . Love one another. . . . Rejoice in the Lord always. Again I will say, rejoice!*

DJ flipped from side to side with each verse. Finally, she sat up in bed and rubbed her eyes. "God, I need to get to sleep so I can get up early to study. I didn't yell at my mother this time—I thought I did pretty well. Anyway, you know I'm trying to control my mouth and my temper. What gives?" She waited, her arms crossed on her raised knees and her good cheek resting on her wrist.

A soft tap at her door made her think, for just an instant, God had arrived to answer her.

"Come in."

Lindy poked her head in and, seeing DJ sitting up, entered the room. "I heard you tossing around. Can't sleep, either?"

Enough light from the streetlights entered the windows that DJ could see her mother's shape but not her expression. At least the tone of voice sounded comforting. She hung on to Lindy's last word. "Either?"

"Yeah, I kept hearing our conversation over and over."

DJ waited. "Me too." She scooted over and patted the bed beside her. "You can sit down if you want."

Lindy sat, one knee up on the bed, so she was partly facing DJ. "That bandage on your face scared me half to pieces."

"Mom, it's no big deal."

"If you had to have stitches, it's going to leave a scar. That *is* a big deal to me."

"The doctor said it would disappear with time. We'll hardly be able to see it."

"The thought of a scar on your face doesn't bother you?"

"Not a whole lot, but then I haven't seen it yet. Jackie changed the bandage. She said a scar like this would have been a badge of honor back in the days of sword fights."

"Great. So my daughter walks down the aisle at my wedding looking like she's been in a duel."

DJ snorted. She could tell from the tone that her mother was poking fun of the idea. "Does it really bother you?"

"Not really. Not as much as the fact that you got hurt and neither Gran nor I were with you. Besides, you can cover the scar up with makeup if you like."

"Mom, you and Gran can't be with me all of my life." Still, her mother's words warmed DJ's insides.

"I know. But cut me some slack, okay? I'm just learning about this mom stuff."

DJ thought a bit. "You know, I see Joe more than Gran nowadays. I miss her, especially in the mornings."

"Funny, she said the same thing the other day." Lindy turned and patted DJ's hands on her knees. "You think you can sleep now?"

"Mm-hmm." DJ could feel her eyelids getting heavy.

"Me too." Lindy stood and leaned over to kiss DJ's cheek. "Mom reminded me that you have a very forgiving heart. I'm glad you do. Sometimes I think you are more grown-up than I am."

"Huh?" *Great, that was an intelligent, mature answer. Try again.*

"Only in some ways, of course."

"Night, Mom. I love you."

"Thank you, Darla Jean Randall." Lindy's voice wore a coat of tears. "Have a good day tomorrow." She sniffed as she went out the door.

DJ snuggled back down in her bed. The words "I love you" had just popped out. Had she ever before said "I love you" to her mother? Gran yes, but to her mother? Not for a few years at least.

"Thank you, heavenly Father," she whispered just before dropping off to sleep.

DJ explained her accident about fifty times at school the next day. Her eye was already turning black, especially underneath. "I look like a raccoon," she muttered to Amy in the washroom after lunch.

"Not really. They have two black eyes and no bandage." Amy brushed her black hair and wrapped a scrunchie around the thick, straight mass. "Did you hear what happened at the Academy this weekend?"

"How would I if you didn't tell me?" DJ turned from examining the bandage and the new zit on her chin.

"Joe might have." Amy stuffed her brush back into her backpack.

"They were too grossed out about my face to think of anything else."

"How come you told Gran not to tell your mother?"

" 'Cause I was afraid she'd freak and probably give my da—Brad—a bad time. And it wasn't his fault. I let Herndon turn out on me. When I think about it, it was probably all my own fault. My timing was off when he ticked it the first time, so then he didn't have confidence in me, and well, he turned out. I shoulda been ready."

"I wouldn't let Bridget hear me say that." Amy headed for the door. "Come on, we'll be late."

"I know—what do you think, I'm stupid or something?"

Amy raised one straight eyebrow.

"Don't answer that." As Amy headed the opposite way, DJ hollered after her, "So what happened at the Academy?"

Amy turned around, walking backward. "Tell you later."

Keeping her mind on her classes the rest of the day wasn't easy.

"So what happened?" DJ pounced with her question as soon as she and Amy met again at their locker.

"Bridget will probably introduce her to you." Amy sorted through her books to decide what to take home.

"Who? Amy Marie Yamamoto, do you want an eye to match mine?"

Amy ducked away and slung her backpack over one shoulder. "Mrs. Lamond Ellsindorf—you-can-call-me-Bunny—that's who." Amy threw a you-really-don't-want-to-know-more look over her shoulder. "To listen to her tell it, she is the most important rider on the East Coast, or was, until her husband got transferred out here to the wilds of California and she was *forced* to come with him."

They climbed into the backseat of the Yamamoto minivan. Amy's older brother, John, who after finally, as he said, turning the big one-six, had just gotten his driver's license, was driving.

"There'll be no comments from the peewee section," he growled.

"John." Mrs. Yamamoto might not be very big, but one word from her, and her children shaped up. "Hi, you two. Ignore the grouch here. DJ, whatever happened to your face?" She turned around to see better.

DJ briefly told her story again, sharing enough to be polite.

"And the wedding coming up, too. What a shame." She turned back to the front. "Now, John, you watch your speed." The implied "this time" made DJ glance curiously at Amy.

She mouthed, "He got a warning ticket." DJ covered her snort with a sneeze.

"So what about that Mrs. What's-her-name?" DJ asked when she could look at Amy without giggling.

"You'll see" was all Amy would say.

DJ was in for a flurry of questions about her new look later at the Academy. "Think I'll just wear a sign that says 'I got dumped' or something," DJ muttered to Major.

He sniffed the bandage and snorted, spraying her with a fine mist. "So you don't like the smell of bandage, huh?" She wiped her face. "Thanks a big fat lot." She leaned against his neck and hugged him, making sure her bandage didn't rub against him. The doctor had said to keep it clean and dry. So far, she'd managed.

Patches, too, gave her the once-over. Instead of snorting, he backed away.

"Oh yeah, anything to act nervous about, you'll take." She snapped a tie shank on his halter and snubbed him down to a stall bar. Patches couldn't be trusted to stand still or keep his teeth to himself while being groomed. She'd learned that the hard way, too.

Once she had him groomed and saddled, she settled in

for a rough ride. "Now, you just behave yourself, and we'll get along fine."

His ears flicked back and forth, letting her know he was listening, but his attention was clearly on a flashy bay taking jumps in the middle of the covered arena.

"Make sure you stay to the outside," Bridget said as she opened the gate to the arena. "Give the jumper plenty of room." She smiled up at DJ. "I am glad you were not hurt worse. Next time, lower the jump after a refusal, then work up to the earlier height. Get your horse's confidence back and yours, too."

"Thanks." *Who blabbed?* she wondered. But when DJ felt Patches hump his back, she put all other thoughts from her mind. Arena sand wasn't one of her favorite meals. She could tell after her warm-up laps that Mrs. Johnson had been riding over the weekend because Patches suddenly figured he could do whatever he wanted. DJ thought otherwise. Their training time was nearly over before he gave up the battle.

"You know, you stubborn beast, we would both have a lot more fun if you'd do what you're told, when you're told."

The next time through, he started, stopped, cantered slow and easy, changed leads, and even backed up with only a flicking of his ears.

"He about used up all your patience?" Bridget swung the gate open to let them out.

"Tried to."

"You do well with him. Mrs. Johnson was asking if you thought he was ready for you to work with the two of them together."

"Me?"

Bridget nodded.

Doing her best to keep her cool and watch Patches at the same time, DJ asked, "What do you think?"

"Until I watched you work him today, I thought any time but . . ."

"He's not usually this much of a pain. She has to learn to make him mind is all."

"I will let her know that you will take her on as a student. She can set up a regular lesson time with you when she is ready. You will be paid double, one hour on him and one coaching them both. Any questions?"

DJ shook her head. "Not now, but later, I bet."

"Good. See you on Megs in—"

"Could you maybe give me half an hour?"

DJ could have groomed six horses in that time, her hands flew so fast. Wait until she told Amy. An adult student!

But in the car, Amy was too busy grumbling to let DJ squeeze a word in edgewise. "That . . . that witch. She thinks she owns the place and that all of us are her slaves!"

After hearing Amy out, DJ asked, "So why does Bridget let her get away with stuff like that?"

Both Joe and Amy shrugged.

"But I'll start asking around," Joe promised. "Something odd is going on here."

DJ had been home an hour before she heard the garage door open and her mother's car pull inside. The meat loaf in the oven smelled good and would be done in half an hour, along with the baked potatoes. Just a few minutes before, DJ had checked everything to make sure nothing was out of place. The house looked good, the dinner smelled better, and DJ had washed and changed clothes.

Tonight, she and her mother would have a good evening together.

"There are two messages on the machine for you," she said while taking the plates down to set the table.

"Thanks, dear. What a day this has been!" Lindy set her briefcase on the counter and slipped off her heels.

"You want a cup of tea?"

"That sounds heavenly. Make it a raspberry zinger, okay?" She punched the code into the machine and scribbled some numbers as she listened. After dialing, she tapped a pearl-tinted fingernail on the countertop.

DJ knew that simple gesture said her mother was feeling worse than she looked. With no lipstick, smeared mascara, and her hair tousled as if she'd raked her fingers through it in frustration, she didn't look like the normally polished Lindy.

After the greeting, Lindy exploded. "What! What do you mean?" A pause. "No, that can't be."

DJ froze. Now what?

Lindy hung up the phone, eyes closed, face twisted as though she were in pain.

"Mom, what's wrong?"

"The Carillion—you know, the place we were planning to have the reception? It burned to the ground last night. Maybe this is the sign I've been afraid would happen. I just knew we'd have to call off the wedding!"

7

"NO, MOM! YOU CAN'T DO THAT!" DJ grabbed her mother's shoulders.

Lindy shrugged her off. "I don't see any alternative. We can't find a place to house the reception this close to the date." She rubbed her forehead. "There are just too many things going wrong."

DJ stared at her mother. *What can I do? God, surely you have a place in mind for the reception. Help!* She waited, hoping for a sign, a clue, anything.

Nothing. Her mind felt as blank as the message board in front of her. At a sound, she turned from studying the blank board to her mother, who now stood with her forehead against a cupboard door, her shoulders shaking. *She's crying. Mom is crying.* DJ started forward and stopped. What could she do?

Quickly, she grabbed the box of tissues from the counter and crossed to her mother. "Here." Her voice came as gently as it did with a flighty foal. "Come on, Mom. Let's go into the other room."

"I . . . I can't h-handle any m-more." Tears streamed down Lindy's face as she pulled a tissue from the proffered box. "Robert will be so disappointed." She blew her nose and wiped her eyes, but within a heartbeat, she was more tear streaked than before. And still the tears kept on.

DJ steered her to the sofa. "Sit." When Lindy collapsed against the soft cushions, DJ took the place beside her. She set the box of tissues on her mother's lap and picked up her shaking hand.

"How about if I call Gran?"

A violent shake of the head met that suggestion. *Robert? Should I call Robert?* No, he lived too far away. *God, you're the only one near enough to help.* She rubbed her mom's shoulder and gently tucked the hair behind her ear. How many times had Gran done the same for her? Loving pats and a soothing tone meant love more than anything else did to DJ. She made herself relax and let her mother cry.

Finally, the downpour changed to a shower, then to a meandering drop. After more nose blowing and eye wiping, Lindy at last laid her hands in her lap, a clump of tissues mounded beside her. She blinked and drew in a deep breath, letting it out in a sigh.

"I really don't think I'm cut out to be a wife and a mother."

"You already *are* a mother—my mother."

"You're right. Then being a wife is the problem."

"No, a place for the reception is the problem." DJ propped her elbows on her knees. "I think Gran and Joe might have an idea where else to look. If nothing else, we can have it in the church basement. Or in the covered arena at the Academy."

"Great. I can see us all dressed up in our fancy clothes, making sure some horse doesn't eat the wedding cake."

DJ blinked. Her mother had made a joke, a good sign. "There's got to be other places to have a reception."

"You may not know this, but I called lots of other places before settling on this one. They were either too expensive or unavailable or . . ."

"Or what?"

"Or . . . I had already chosen the Carillion." Lindy rubbed her tongue over her lower lip. "I think I gave the list to Gran."

DJ could see the wheels start turning again. "You want me to call Robert for you and tell him the wedding is off?" DJ couldn't resist the urge to tease her mother even if it might prove to be the dumbest thing she'd ever done.

Lindy rolled her swollen red eyes. "Not yet anyway." She blew her nose again. "Maybe I just needed a good cry."

"M-o-t-h-e-r."

"Well, a cry sometimes releases pent-up stress and—"

The phone rang. DJ crossed to the table next to the wing chair and picked up the cordless phone. "Hi, this is DJ."

"Hi yourself." Robert's voice sounded as tired as Lindy's. "Your mom there?"

"I . . . ah, just a minute." DJ buried the phone against her shoulder. "It's Robert," she whispered. "You want to call him back?"

Lindy shook her head. "No, I'll take it." She sniffed. "Is something burning?"

"Burning? Yikes, the meat loaf!" DJ handed the phone to her mother and dashed for the kitchen. Grabbing a potholder, she pulled open the oven. Smoke billowed up in her face, making her eyes sting and a cough erupt. At least there were no flames. She opened the window above the sink, gulping in the fresh air. From here, she could hear her mother talking in the family room, her tone sounding almost normal again. DJ returned to the open oven, where the apples she'd set in a bread pan now sat in a crust of smoking burnt sugar. All the water had evaporated.

She pulled the pan from the oven and set it on another hot pad. "I guess the apples don't look too terrible if we don't eat the black stuff," she told herself as she turned off the oven and took out the meat loaf, now dark brown on the bottom. She placed the crusty baked potatoes on the counter along side of it. So much for a perfect dinner, but then this wasn't turning into a perfect night anyway.

DJ went ahead and fixed her plate, taking it to the dining room. The two place settings now looked forlorn at the end and side of the long table. She thought of the meals eaten here with Gran and Gramps and Mom long ago, and lately with Robert and the boys. The room had seemed so full of life those other times, but now the silence hovered like a ghostly presence that snuffed out sounds.

Surely Robert could talk some sense into her mother.

But where *could* they hold the reception? The next phone call had to be to Gran, that was for sure. She would come up with an answer, like always. Of course, Gran came up with answers because she always prayed about them first. God sure seemed to listen to Gran's prayers.

Did that mean He *didn't* listen to hers? DJ thoughtfully poured ketchup on her meat loaf. No, God had answered her prayers many times, too—Gran would say all the time, adding that sometimes DJ just didn't like His answers. So what was God saying now?

She heard her mother dialing the phone. From the conversation, DJ knew her mother and Gran were talking. She picked up her plate and fork and wandered into the family room, sitting in the wing chair. Her mother nodded to her and kept on talking. A frown would have meant DJ should leave the room.

When Lindy pushed the off button and laid down the phone, she looked over at her daughter. "You were right. We . . . *I* won't cancel the wedding. This is a challenge, not a conclusion."

DJ could feel her smile widening with every word. "Way to go, Mom. You aren't a quitter."

"No, I'm not. And neither are you." Lindy closed her eyes and shook her head. "Not that quitting didn't sound real inviting a while ago." She looked up again after studying her hands, clasped casually on her knees. "What is it that smells burnt?"

"The baked apples. The rest of the dinner is on the stove." DJ could feel her appetite coming back. "You want me to fix you a plate?"

"I think I'll go change first. I feel like a wrung-out dishrag. I'll eat later and put the food away."

"Guess that means I can get to my homework right away." DJ took her plate back to the kitchen, then looked over her shoulder. "You okay?"

"I am now—or will be. I guess we could have the reception here or over at Gran's if need be. So it would be crowded. So what?"

DJ and her mother walked up the stairs together, arms around each other's waist.

Several hours later when DJ turned out her light, she went to stand at the window to watch the mist rainbowing in the streetlights. Weddings, floods, fires, new fathers—what else could happen?

The next afternoon, DJ met the new woman at the Academy.

"Put that pole back up."

DJ turned from her teaching position at the far end of the arena where she had her three students circling to leave space for the jumper.

"I think she's talking to you," Angie Lincoln said as she trotted past DJ.

"Who?"

"That lady."

"I said, put that pole back up." The woman on the light chestnut horse flung the words over her shoulder as she cantered past and headed for another jump.

DJ signaled to the girls to keep circling and crossed the sandy space to set the rail back up on the standards. *Who does this woman think she is?* DJ swallowed the rest of the thought before she could get any more worked up than she already was. Stalking back to her class, she pasted a smile on her face.

"Okay, kids, lope now and watch your leads." DJ felt unfriendly eyes drill a stare into her back. She heard another tick, but this time, there was no thud of a falling pole. She watched her students intently, making comments as needed and cheering them on. Krissie, her blue eyes glacial, kept sending icy looks in the jumper's direction.

"Come on, kids, concentrate on your horse and what you are doing." DJ let them make another round before signaling them to join her in the center of their circle. "Okay, you did good, like you always do. Good enough to move on. Let's start working on backing up so we can begin opening gates pretty soon. I know you all plan on trail-riding, and that class calls for opening and going through a gate."

Angie raised her hand. "I already know how to back up. Want to see?"

DJ nodded.

Angie pulled back on her reins. "Back." She clucked at the same time. "Come on, back." Her horse shook his head but did as asked. Backing slowly, he angled toward the horse on his left.

"Good. Anyone else?" The other two shook their heads.

DJ had them all dismount and showed them how to hold the reins and push against their horse's shoulder, giving the back-up command at the same time. She helped each girl, reminding them all to praise their horses and pat them for doing right. After the ground work, they mounted, and again she helped each one, herself on the ground and her students in the saddle.

Sam's horse kept shaking his head and playing with his bit. He did not want to back up for anything. DJ persisted, reminding Sam, "After squeezing, you have to lean forward slightly to open the door so he can back up." The horse gave in and stepped back. DJ looked up at the grin on the girl's face.

"See, you just have to be patient."

"And stubborn." Sam, short for Samantha, leaned forward and patted her horse's neck. "Good boy."

DJ smiled up at the girl. "You did a great job of keeping your cool, kiddo."

"I'm learning." Sam tightened her reins as her horse tried to go forward. "Whoa."

When the lesson was over, DJ followed the girls to the barn to make sure they untacked their horses properly. She refused to even look at the woman still working her horse over the jumps, now with one of the other student workers adjusting the bars. Her tone held no more kindness than before. *Has the woman never learned to at least say please?*

That night, Robert and the boys arrived loaded down with boxes of Chinese food for dinner. DJ was setting the table when the phone rang. Because she was closest, Lindy answered it.

DJ looked up when her mother's voice turned extra polite. Pausing in the doorway, she waited.

"Yes, Brad, I have a moment." Lindy paused. "I see."

If only she could hear the other side of the conversation. DJ itched to run for the other phone.

"So you're saying you'd like DJ to attend a horse show with you and Jackie a week from Thursday."

DJ clenched her hands to her sides. *Oh, please, Mom, say yes*.

"I'll have to give this some thought. With the wedding coming up . . . well, how about if I get back to you tomorrow?"

DJ could feel her shoulders slump.

"DJ, we's hungry," Bobby and Billy announced as one.

She set the plates in front of each of them and reached for a carton of sweet-and-sour prawns, the boys' favorite. She tried to listen over their chatter, without success. "Shhh!" She glared at them.

Their mouths turned to Os, and they shrank back as if she'd hit them.

"DJ, was that necessary?" Robert's voice held more than a trace of anger.

8

DJ FELT AS IF SHE'D BEEN STRUCK.

Two lower lips quivered as the Double Bs looked first to their father and then back to DJ.

"I'm sorry, guys." She hunkered down between the two of them and wrapped an arm around each boy. "Please forgive me?"

With four arms strangling her neck, DJ fought back the hot moisture burning behind her eyes.

"I forgive you." The blue eyes on the right said more than the words.

"Me too." The one on the left wriggled in his chair. "'Cause we loves you."

The words rang in DJ's mind long after the boys had left and Robert had given her a hug that said the same.

Is that what would make this family possible? Was there enough love for Brad and Jackie, too?

When she told her grandmother her worries the next afternoon after her stint at the Academy, DJ just shook her head. "Just like you all these years, Gran. How come something so simple as being a family is so hard to live out?"

Gran stroked DJ's hair as DJ leaned against her grandmother's knee. "It is so simple to love, yet sometimes we get in the way of it. Mostly because we want our own way, I guess. Remember, simple and easy aren't the same."

"I want Mom to let me go to the horse show with Brad and Jackie. It would be so cool to see her compete, and Lord Byron is an awesome horse." DJ sat still for a few moments. "Did Robert tell you that I hollered at the boys?"

"No."

"I hurt their feelings, so he yelled at me, and that hurt *my* feelings." She sighed, a deep sigh that started way down and worked its way up. "What a mess. And all because I wanted to hear what Mom was saying to Brad." She turned to give her grandmother one of those I-blew-it half grins. "Of course, listening in would have been eavesdropping, and how many times have you warned me against that?"

Gran put gentle hands on both sides of DJ's face and kissed her forehead from above. "More than once, my dear, more than once."

"More than once what?" Joe ambled into the room, his glasses pushed up on his forehead. "You seen my book, Mel? I can't find it anywhere."

"Which one?"

"The one about training a roping horse. I wanted to show DJ a picture in it." He looked over the room.

"Did you check the bookshelf?"

He shrugged and winked at DJ. "Now, why didn't I think of that?"

DJ and Gran laughed together as he left the room. When he called to report he'd found the book, they laughed again.

When Lindy came to pick up DJ later, she accepted the

offered cup of coffee and took a place at the table. "So, Mother, what did you find?"

"How does the Oak House sound?"

"Really?" Lindy set her coffee down with a thump. "That's perfect. Even closer to the church and—"

"And it costs less, if you can believe it. I know for a fact their food is better than the Carillion's, too."

"And it *is* bigger." Lindy reached a hand across to her mother. "I can't believe it."

DJ felt like she was at a tennis match, swiveling her head between the two. "So God did good, huh?"

Lindy looked at her daughter, then slowly nodded her head. "Yes, He did."

DJ and Gran shared a secret smile. Lindy was coming around.

When Brad called later that evening, DJ answered the phone. "Looks like Major's leg is finally okay," she said when he asked about her horse. "I get to ride him for a brief warm-up tomorrow, then add more time each day. One of these days, the rain will let up for more than a couple of hours at a time and we'll get to use the jumping arena again.

"Speaking of jumping, have you heard of a woman named Mrs. Lamond Ellsindorf? Most people call her Bunny."

"Yes, I think so. Why?"

DJ went on to tell him about the woman's rudeness and how all the academy kids already hated her. "She never says please or thank you. Just orders us around like we're her slaves."

"Hmm. That doesn't sound like the woman we met. I'll ask Jackie and let you know when I pick you up a week from tomorrow. You'll be ready, right?"

"You mean I get to go?"

"That's what your mother said when she called me today. She didn't tell you?"

"Nope, we were talking about the new reception place. Guess she forgot."

"You'll need some dressy casual clothes, like a blazer or a good sweater."

"Sure." She mentally inventoried her clothes closet. She'd outgrown the one outfit she kept for special events. "I'll be ready. Thanks, Da—Brad." She hung up, wondering at her slip of the tongue. Was she really beginning to think of him as Dad?

Later, after an hour at her books, DJ got a black cherry soda from the refrigerator and sat down beside her mother on the sofa. "Thanks for letting me go to the horse show."

"You're welcome. Robert and I agree that it will be a good experience for you."

DJ figured she owed Robert a big thank-you. She picked at the cuticle on her thumb, then took a swallow of the soda. *How can I ask for another favor?* "When do we go pick up the dresses for the wedding?"

"I don't know. I should call, I guess." Lindy looked up from reading the paper. "Why?"

"Well, I need some nice clothes for the trip."

Lindy looked at her daughter thoughtfully. "Yes, you do. It's time you began to develop a style of your own."

"I don't need a whole wardrobe." DJ started to say something else, then thought the better of it. "I . . . I thought maybe a tailored jacket of some kind or something. Mine are all for the show-ring."

Lindy folded the newspaper and placed it on the table.

"Let's go see what you have that might work and make a list of what you need."

DJ groaned to herself. *Leave it to my mother to make a production out of it. All I want is a blazer.* But by the time they'd finished, she was almost looking forward to the shopping trip. Almost.

Thursday poured its way into the Bay area. Water sheeted the whole street, not just the gutters and drains, when Mrs. Yamamoto drove the kids to school. At times, the windshield wipers couldn't clear the glass fast enough, and they were nearly late, the traffic was moving so slowly.

The low places between the buildings looked like miniature lakes as the students slogged from building to building. The outside lockers gave the rain another chance at the kids. DJ kept all her books in her backpack so she didn't have to stand and fight with her combination.

"What a yucky day!" She bailed into the van as soon as Amy shoved open the back door. John was already in the front seat, a frown on his face because he wasn't getting to drive.

"Just don't ask again, John," Mrs. Yamamoto cautioned. "Hi, girls. DJ, Joe called to say he and some of the other retired police were going up north of here to help fill sandbags. He wants you to take care of Ranger for him."

"Sure."

"Can you be ready in half an hour? I can't think that anyone will ride in weather like this."

"All right." DJ looked at Amy, who hadn't said a word so far. "What's wrong? You sick?"

Amy nodded. "I think I'm going to throw up." She suddenly sat up very straight. "Mom! Quick, stop the car!"

In spite of the rain, Amy hung her head out the van door

and heaved. When she finally sat back in the seat, DJ handed her a napkin. "You look terrible."

"Thanks." Amy leaned her head back and closed her eyes.

"You going to make it home now?" Mrs. Yamamoto turned to check on her daughter. "Looks like you'll have another horse to take care of, DJ. Unless John—"

"No time. I have to be at Dad's. It's my day to work."

"No problem. I'll do it." DJ put her hand on Amy's shoulder. "You cold?"

"F-fr-freezing." Amy wrapped both arms around her middle. "I knew I shoulda called home earlier, but . . . well . . ."

Her last words disappeared on the wind as DJ threw open the door and bailed out. The wild wind tried to blow her back in, but she slammed the door shut and headed for the front door, digging in her pocket for the key. Why hadn't she thought to get it out earlier? A branch had blown off the oak tree in the front yard, flattening the snowball bush beside it.

Even standing under the porch roof, DJ was battered by the wind, which blew rain down her neck. The downspouts sounded like waterfalls, and the heavy drops hammered the glass, sheeting the windows in their rush downward. DJ huddled deeper in her slicker until she finally inserted the key in the lock.

The house felt damp and empty, as if lonely huddling against the storm. DJ picked up the phone to call Gran, realizing that the power was off since the light on the answering machine glowed neither green nor red. At least the kitchen phone still worked.

"Hi. Mrs. Yamamoto is taking me to the Academy, but Amy is sick. Could you please pick me up afterward?"

"Sure will. You have power over there?"

"Nope."

"I'm afraid we're in the same boat, but I have the fireplace going so we can roast hot dogs for dinner. Leave a note for your mother. On second thought, you get ready, and I'll call. Bring your stuff to spend the night if the power doesn't come back on."

DJ did her chores and Amy's, too. Because of the rain driving in from the west, the horses stabled in the open stalls were drenched in spite of the roof. Water ran down the aisle to where one of the men had trenched it off to the sides before it could run into the barn. Since so many people couldn't make it to the Academy, it was already growing dark outside by the time the stalls were cleaned and the horses fed and groomed. Due to the power outage, Bridget had closed the ring, so no one was riding.

DJ and Tony Andrada stood back from the door, watching the rain sheet across the parking area.

"This is about as bad as the hurricanes where I came from." Tony shook his head. "If I never see one of those suckers again, it'll be too soon. And here I thought California had good weather."

DJ rubbed her cold hands together. She should have brought gloves, but whoever heard of wearing gloves because of cold California weather? She did have riding gloves, but she only wore them when she had to.

"You had a chance to help the Queen yet?" DJ asked Tony. Mrs. Ellsindorf had earned her nickname.

"I stay out of her way. Seems to work."

"Lucky you!" Just then Gran drove in and parked right in front of the door. "See ya." DJ dashed outside again, duffel and backpack in hand. The wind slammed the car door shut for her, barely missing her leg.

"I can't imagine what it's like for those people helping

sandbag." Gran peered through the brief clearing made by the wipers. "You better be praying for your grandfather and his crew up there while I drive us home."

"You heard from him?"

"Nope." They nearly had to shout to be heard above the rain, the heater, and the wipers.

DJ sent her prayers heavenward, including one for her mother and every other unlucky person on the roads.

As they drove past Robert's new house, DJ glanced over—just in time to see a chunk of the roof lift off and roll across the yard.

9

"GRAN, STOP! THE ROOF!"

"I'm not stopping here. I'm getting us home and in the house as fast as I can. We'll call Robert when we get there." They both ducked instinctively as a branch, broken off a tree just ahead, sailed straight at them, then slid across the roof.

DJ gripped the door handle. *What is happening at the barns? I know Gran won't go back tonight. God, please, keep Major safe. And help us to get home safely, too. We have only a little way to go now.*

As Gran turned the station wagon into her driveway, they heard a loud crack. Straight ahead, the pine tree behind the garage crashed forward, splintering one side of the garage as it fell. Electric wires leaped and fluttered, coming to rest across the driveway.

"Two more seconds, and we'd have been right there." Gran pointed to where the lines lay. The garage settled into a tilt that made it look like a toy a child had bashed. "Thank you, heavenly Father, for keeping us safe. And for taking our power away earlier."

"Amen." DJ breathed the word. Her heart still felt as if it would leap right out of her chest and flutter to the ground like the wires had. She peered out, the falling darkness more pronounced without streetlights. "You think you still have a phone?"

Gran turned off the ignition. "Possibly. Those lines are buried underground. Joe kept saying he wanted to trench and bury our electric lines, too, but somehow we didn't get to it."

"Not like you guys haven't been busy or anything." DJ shot her grandmother a look of love. Gran's face gleamed stark white in the reflection from the headlights, and her normally strong hands shook as she flicked off the interior light.

"The car could have been in the garage. *We* could have been in the garage, just getting out. Oh, DJ, I am so grateful." Tears formed at the edges of her eyes. "God is so good to us." Gran brushed the drops away. "Let's head for the house. You wait a minute until I get the door unlocked."

"How about if I unlock the door and you wait?"

Gran snorted. "I don't think so. My hand will quit shaking enough to insert the key."

DJ held hers up. "Then you're in better shape than me." They held up matching hands, hands that trembled in spite of their best efforts to keep them still.

"The rest of me feels just the same." Gran tucked her purse under her arm. "Time to get our evening shower." She shoved open the car door, fighting the wind that howled against it. When she stepped free, the door slammed on its own.

DJ waited until Gran got to the door, then bolted from the car. Running to the house was like leaning into a solid wall—an invisible wall that nearly dropped her on her face when it huffed, then blew her backward. If, as Tony had said, this storm felt almost like a hurricane, DJ had no desire to research the difference.

Once inside, the howling wind was muted enough by

the snug house that DJ and Gran could at least talk in normal voices.

"I'm in the kitchen," Gran called. The flare of a just lit kerosene lamp warmed the way for DJ. "Looks like we're going to have to play pioneers," Gran said as she lit another. "I can remember my mother talking about lamplight when she was a girl and how it was more flattering."

DJ knew Gran had grown up in the South on a farm. She and Gramps had moved to California after he had been stationed there during his term in the navy. One of Gran's sisters still lived on the home place, as they called it, but she refused to visit California. Scared to death of earthquakes, Gran always said with a laugh. At one time, the barn on the home place had been destroyed by a tornado, but only Gran saw the humor in that. As for DJ, she didn't have a whole lot of patience for or interest in her Southern relatives. It was hard to care about people you'd never met.

She shucked off her slicker and shook her head, wet hair whipping her stinging cheeks.

"Land, child, get in the shower while we still have hot water. You take one bathroom, and I'll take the other."

"The fire needs more wood first," DJ said. "Maybe I better bring in a stack before I dry off."

"Good idea. We can set it by the back door to dry. If you dig down a layer or two, it shouldn't be so wet. Joe has it covered, but nothing will stay dry in driving rain like this." Gran glanced at the clock, grimaced, and checked her watch. "I sure wish he were home. What must it be like up on the river?"

DJ shuddered. Surely they had ordered the workers into buildings to protect them. She pulled her wet slicker back on and headed for the back door. The wind tore at the door, but DJ managed to get it open. The storm door was another matter. The wind grabbed it and slammed it against the wall so hard, the glass shattered and the aluminum frame bent.

"Don't worry about that!" Gran hollered over the wind. "Hand the wood to me and I'll stack it. Careful!"

Within a few minutes, the laundry room took on a new purpose. Instead of being used to wash and dry clothes, wood was stacked everywhere—on the floor, the dryer, the washer, and in the deep double sink. They moved the last loads right into the family room and stacked them on papers out of the way along one wall.

Gran answered the phone as DJ returned with one last load.

"I don't know how bad it was," she was saying when DJ entered the kitchen. "DJ is the one who saw the roof go. I didn't dare take my eyes off the road."

DJ hung up both their slickers in the laundry room and left her boots there, too. Her jeans felt like she'd gone swimming in them.

"Robert says thanks for letting him know about the roof but that there's nothing to be done until the storm abates. They've closed all the bridges across the Bay, so he's stuck in the city. He said he wouldn't ask his local crew to come over, either." She trailed a finger across her chin, then shook her head. "I know worrying about Joe won't help a bit but . . ." She reached out to rub DJ's shoulder.

"You always say to put people in the Lord's hands and leave them there."

"I'm tryin', darlin'. You have no idea how hard I'm tryin'."

The deepening of her grandmother's Southern accent told DJ how upset her grandmother was. Wishing she could do more, she wrapped both arms around Gran's shoulders and hugged. The two rocked together, sharing comfort in the lamplight, an oasis in the midst of the storm.

Lindy called later to say she was fine. She and a bunch of co-workers were holed up at the office, where they still had power. The cafe on the first floor of the building was doing gangbuster business, trying to feed all the stranded. She had no idea when she'd be home.

DJ and Gran went back to their cozy picnic in front of the fireplace. When the phone rang again, they looked at each other, hope blazoned across their faces. Tears spurted as soon as Gran heard the deep voice on the line.

"Oh, darlin', I was so worried about you." Gran wiped her nose on the back of her hand, making DJ laugh. She handed her grandmother a box of tissues. "No, we're fine—warm and dry, thanks to the fireplace. We haven't had power for hours. You're the one who we've been worried about." She nodded while he talked.

"Tell him I love him," DJ said. Gran nodded again.

After hanging up, Gran relaxed against the padded chair, her arms around her knees. She took the crispy marshmallow off the fork that DJ extended. "Perfect. They moved the volunteers to a school until the storm calms down enough for travel to be safe. Right now there are too many falling trees by the river, so only emergency vehicles are out on the roads." The phone rang again.

"Why, Brad, thank you for calling. Yes, we're fine. DJ and I are piggin' out on hot dogs and marshmallows in front of a fire. That's right, no power. Sure, here she is." Gran handed DJ the phone.

"Hi. How are things up your way?" DJ inquired.

"The levee is holding, so we're safe so far. The other rivers are much worse than the Petaluma. All the horses are in the barns or loose in the arena. Of course, the power's out, but that's not the important thing right now. With my luck, that mare will foal tonight."

"Really?"

"No, I don't think so. She promised to wait for you."

"I hope so." She told him where the others were stranded. "A pine tree fell on Gran's garage, and a chunk of the roof blew off the house Robert is remodeling, but we're okay. I've never been out in such a storm in my life." When she hung up, she put another marshmallow on her fork. "Burned or brown?"

"Brown, as in dark." Gran fluffed her hair and stretched back against the chair. "How come I feel like it's the middle of the night?"

"Got me." DJ blew on the marshmallow she'd gotten too close to the fire. "Guess this one is mine." She drew off the outer coating and returned the gooey rest to the fire. "You want me to get out the sleeping bags?"

"No, I think our beds will be warm enough. I'll just come out and put more wood in the fire once in a while." They both listened, suddenly aware of the quiet. "The wind has died down. Thank you, God."

DJ nibbled on the marshmallow as she went to look out the window. Rain still sluiced down, but at least the roar of water and wind was gone. She thought about asking Gran if they could drive over to the Academy but knew the answer without wasting her breath. If only she'd thought to call Bridget before it got so late. Wouldn't the academy owner call them if something was wrong?

The rain had stopped during the night, and the clouds had blown away. The sun rose again as if the horrible storm was a thing of everyone's imagination. Much to DJ's disgust, they had school as usual since the power came back on during the night, too.

After helping her feed and water the horses, Gran drove DJ to school in the morning. Amy was still home sick. *I can tell this is going to be a really great day*, DJ grumbled to herself. *If I'd known Amy was sick, I could at least have fed Josh*. Other than mushy stalls, the Academy had weathered the storm all right, certainly better than Gran's garage.

DJ had a hard time keeping her mind on her classes. She would rather have been home helping Gran clean up the branches from the fallen tree. *Wait till Joe and Robert see the mess—they'll have a fit*.

Her afternoon went to pot when her algebra teacher called for a quiz. DJ took out paper and pencil, making sure she had a good eraser. She'd done the homework, but still . . . a quiz today?

"I hate algebra," she muttered before the teacher called for silence. The guy across the aisle muttered with her. She looked up at the problems on the board. *If* $x=3$ *. . .*

She could feel her head begin to fuzz up, so she forced her mind to concentrate on the numbers and letters on the board. But when the teacher called time and said to hand your paper to the person behind you, she knew there were at least two wrong out of the ten. She hadn't even gotten to them.

She ended up with four wrong and barely a passing grade. If her mother found out, she might say no to the horse show. Granted, her total grade at the end of the quarter wouldn't be totally dependent on four mistakes, but this hadn't been the first time she'd blown a quiz.

When she school day finally ended, DJ slunked into the rear seat of the Yamamoto van. John was driving again, whistling and tapping the steering wheel, waiting for her.

"Will you take care of Josh tonight, DJ?" he asked. "I need to get to work right away."

"Sure." She turned to Mrs. Yamamoto. "How's Amy?"

"It turns out she has bronchitis on top of a flu bug, so

it'll be a few days before she can come back to school. I took her to the doctor this morning. The antibiotics he prescribed will help soon."

"Is she coughing her head off?"

"Sure is. And not having power yesterday didn't help. She was so cold we brought her down to sleep by the fireplace."

"I'll ride my bike to the Academy," DJ said when she got out of the car and waved. "Tell Amy I'll call her later."

As John backed out the driveway, she had a brainstorm—maybe John would help her with algebra. He was a numbers genius. Computer genius, too.

She went into the house, still thinking about algebra. Probably there was a computer program that could help her understand this stuff. She stacked the few dishes in the dishwasher, threw a load of her things in the wash, and headed for the Academy. Her mother had been home to change clothes but hadn't even left a message. Now what was going on?

No classes today, read the sign posted on the duties board. And here she'd just been able to ride Major again. Did that mean she couldn't work Patches, either? DJ checked in Bridget's office, but no one was there. The arena stood empty.

The place felt about as deserted as her own home. Where was everyone?

DJ went into the barn knowing she had to take care of at least three horses. Dirty stalls called to her. She got some carrots out of the refrigerator and, breaking them into small pieces, filled her pockets. Retrieving the wheelbarrow and manure fork, she waved to Hilary Jones, who was grooming her horse in the other aisle, and made her way to Major's stall.

Major leaned against the stall bars, stretching to greet her. His nose quivered in a soundless nicker, his ears nearly touching at the tips.

"Hi, fella, you had a lonely day without a visit from GJ?" She fed him a carrot and tickled the whisker brush on his upper lip. Ranger stuck his head out over the bars of his stall and tossed his head, demanding a treat, too.

"Hey, stuff it, kid. I'll get to you in a minute."

Ranger nickered again, even more demanding this time, including a stamp of one front foot.

"What a spoiled brat you are." She gave Major another treat and rubbed up behind his ears. "You should give him lessons in manners, you know." Major rubbed his forehead against the front of her jacket and nosed her pockets for more carrot. "Be back in a minute."

She gave him a pat and walked the few steps to Ranger's gate. "Now, see here."

Ranger tossed his head, his forelock and mane flopping with the action.

DJ gave him a carrot chunk and scratched his cheek while he chewed. "Does Joe give you whatever you want? You seem like a hopeless case." Ranger snuffled her hands, then her pockets. "Oh, so you know where we keep the stuff, do you?" She gave him another treat and stepped back, her hands on her hips. "That rain sure soaked your bedding. I better bring in tons of shavings or you'll be standing in the mud."

She tied Major in the aisle and began forking the wet and dirty shaving and straw mixture into the wheelbarrow. Only minutes passed before she removed her Windbreaker and hung it over a bar. She'd become spoiled herself with Joe cleaning the stalls weekday mornings. She wiped the sweat from her forehead and trundled the barrow to dump, refill, and dump again. When she was down to bare, wet ground, she headed for the shavings pile and dumped several loads on the bare floor of the stall. She made it plenty deep before spreading a layer of straw on top of that.

If it ever rained like that again, she could hang plastic on the outside wall to keep the rain from soaking the dirt in the stall. She decided to mention it to Bridget when they had time.

She brought Major back in his stall and began on Ranger's. On a trek to the ramp where they dumped the dirty bedding, she heard Bridget's voice coming from the stalls on the opposite side of the area. "At least someone is here," she told Ranger when he nickered for another treat.

When both horses had clean stalls, she refilled the water buckets and hung hay in each net before doing the same for Amy's horse. After putting the wheelbarrow and things away, she picked up the grooming bucket and, starting with Josh, groomed all three horses.

She found Bridget up on the roof with a hammer and nails. One of the stable workers was with her on the roof, and another was handing up sheets of corrugated fiberglass roofing to be nailed in place.

"If you want extra work, you can help." Bridget finished nailing off a section, then stood and kneaded the middle of her back with her fists.

DJ wanted to ask why *she* was up there but kept her mouth closed. "I'm not much of a help with a hammer, but if you have other stuff to do, I can maybe handle that."

"I would rather you not ride in the arena today since some of the roofing is loose and could come down." Bridget helped slide the next roofing panel in place. "So if your stalls are clean and the horses cared for, that is all for the day." She smiled down at DJ. "Thank you for the offer to help, but I think we have it under control."

"See you." DJ turned to go and saw Mrs. Ellsindorf

coming their way. The woman's face was permanently carved into a frowning glare. She passed without an acknowledgment of any kind, as though DJ wasn't even on the same planet with her, let alone the same aisle.

Well, hello to you, too—and I hope you have a nice day. DJ saw Hilary coming toward her, shaking her head.

"We sure get some interesting people around here." Hilary set the wheelbarrow down and took the fork to load shavings.

"Interesting—is that what you call her?"

"Well, not quite, but you've got to at least try to be polite, you know."

"That's what Gran says, too." DJ shook her head. "But why is she so mad all the time?"

"I imagine not being able to ride in the arena ticked her off today. I wish she'd ride in the morning so we didn't have to make way for her. Guess no one told her the afternoons are left to us kids." Hilary forked the shavings as she talked.

"Maybe she has a job or something." DJ looked out to where Bridget had come off the roof to talk with the woman.

"Maybe." Hilary's tone said she didn't believe it for a second.

"Well, see ya." DJ headed back to Major's stall to check his leg before she left. Even if he didn't need the ice packs anymore, a rubbing with liniment wouldn't hurt.

After she'd parked her bike in the garage, she shucked her boots at the bootjack by the back door and entered the kitchen. The blinking light on the answering machine caught her attention, and she pushed the play button.

"DJ, Robert and the boys are coming out around five so we can go over to the house and inspect the damage. Could you take care of Bobby and Billy for a while? Robert said he'd bring dinner." DJ nodded as she waited for the next message.

"DJ, Joe called to ask if you would take care of Ranger for him. He said he'd be home later tonight and he'll do tomorrow as usual. I had hoped to catch you before you left. Call me if there's a problem."

"Already done, Gran," DJ said as she poked the rewind switch. She went upstairs to change into clean clothes, then checked to make sure things were picked up. Since all seemed to be in order, she took the cordless phone and a can of soda to Gran's old chair, where she sat with both legs over one arm while she dialed Amy.

"She's taking a bath," Mrs. Yamamoto said after answering. "Can she call you back?"

"Sure." DJ hung up and dialed Gran's number. After reassuring her grandmother that the horses were cared for, DJ asked, "You want me to come over tomorrow and help clean up the mess around there?"

"No thanks, darlin'. Joe says we have to let the insurance adjuster see the damage first so we can turn in our claim. We'll probably make up a work party this weekend. Do you want to go shopping tonight for your jacket and things?"

"Can't. I've got the Double Bs while Mom and Robert inspect the damage to the house and figure out what to do. How about tomorrow night?"

"We'll see. Y'all want to come here for dinner?"

"Thanks, but Robert is bringing it." DJ went on to tell her the news of the day, making a joke out of the sour look on Mrs. Ellsindorf's face. "I think she practices looking mad and bad."

"She must be a terribly unhappy person."

"Now, don't you go getting any ideas." DJ swung her feet

and let them thud against the chair. "She's not my problem, and I don't have to like her."

"Seems to me like she needs a lot of prayer."

DJ sighed. "Why did I ever bring her up? Gran, you pray for her if you want to, but I'd rather you prayed for me to do better in algebra. Why do I need to learn the stuff?"

After hanging up, DJ headed back upstairs to start her homework. She had a book report due the next week and hadn't begun to read the book yet. She flopped down on her bed on her stomach, Jennie McGrady Mystery in hand. She began reading as she munched on an apple, her feet scissoring the air. Soon, she was so caught up in the book she didn't even know her mother had come home until Lindy stuck her head in the door.

"Hi, DJ, doing your homework?"

"Yup. Gotta get ahead." DJ rolled over enough to see her mother. "You look beat."

"Thanks. Even though they put us up at the hotel last night, I didn't get much sleep with that storm raging outside. Then I had an appointment at eight, so I just changed clothes here and left again. I sure wish I had time to crash for a bit. . . ." She checked her watch. "If they arrive before I get out of the shower, you entertain them, okay?"

DJ nodded and went back to her book.

The fried chicken and fixings Robert brought disappeared in record time. He and Lindy left DJ and the boys to clean up. "You guys mind DJ now."

"We will." They wore their cherub look. " 'Bye, Daddy."

DJ played Go Fish with them for a while, then said, "Look, guys, I'd love to keep playing, but I have a ton of homework to do for Monday, and it won't get done unless I start on it now. How about I set you up with crayons and some paper for coloring while I study?"

" 'Kay. Then will you play horsie?"

DJ groaned. "I guess so. But first you have to be quiet." She led the way up the stairs to her room and set them on the floor with their crayons and papers. Back on her bed, she returned to the world of Jennie McGrady.

"Daddy's here!" The shout jolted her back to her own room.

Papers flew as the boys leaped to their feet and bolted out the door.

DJ blinked as she surveyed the scattered mess. Her blue notebook lay on the floor next to her drawing pad. Pages of each mixed with the paper she'd given the boys for drawing. Her heart thudded—one of them had colored on one of her pictures of the foal!

Her mood darkening, she rummaged through the papers. They'd used others of her drawings for coloring, too, and her algebra papers now wore colored streaks, wavy lines, and circles.

"Bobby and Billy!" DJ hit the stairs running, fury flaming red before her eyes.

10

"HEY, DJ, YOU DON'T HAVE TO yell at them like that." Robert looked up from hugging his boys.

"But they colored on my drawings!" DJ thrust the messy sheets at him. "Look."

"DJ, don't talk like that to Robert!" Lindy turned from hanging up her coat. "What is the matter with you?"

"They ruined my drawings of the filly—the ones Gran said are the best I've ever done."

Robert took the sheets of drawing paper from her hand, glancing from them down at the Double Bs, who wore expressions of total confusion mixed in with sorrow and a bit of fear. Lindy crossed to investigate the damage, too.

"DJ said to color so she could study." One twin thrust out his lower lip.

"We was quiet." A tear bobbled on a set of long eyelashes.

"Can you do the drawings over, DJ?" Robert asked quietly.

"That isn't the point here!" Lindy huffed. "Darla Jean Randall, *you* were the one in charge. That makes *you* responsible if something goes wrong. After all, you agreed to watch the boys." Lindy advanced on her daughter.

DJ clamped her teeth together and glared at her mother.

"Didn't you?"

What could DJ do but nod? *But why couldn't the Bs keep to the stuff I gave them to do?* "They still shouldn't have gotten into my drawings." She crossed her arms over her chest. Maybe if she squeezed hard enough, she could keep the ugliness inside.

Rotten, nosy little brats. All that hard work gone to waste. And she'd thought to frame one for Brad. At least *he* cared about her drawings. He loved them.

She glared again at the twins, steeling herself against their tears.

"I'm talking to you, Darla Jean."

"I hear you. What do you want me to do, fall on my knees and apologize? They"—she stabbed her finger at the boys—"should apologize to me." She jabbed her chest with the same finger.

"DJ, don't talk to your mother that way." Robert cut into their growing fight.

"Stay out of this, Robert. This is between me and DJ." Lindy flashed him a look that would send most people scrambling.

"Now, honey." Robert dropped his voice and tried to sound soothing.

As if that isn't the oldest trick in the book. It won't work with her, either. DJ felt her jaw go even more rigid—if that were possible.

By now, both boys were sobbing. At the sight of them, DJ felt tears gather behind her own eyes. She squinted at her mother. "It wasn't my fault! You always think everything is my fault and that I never do things right. I'm never home on time, I'm—"

"That's enough!" Robert thundered, cutting the air with his hand as though separating the chaotic group.

Four sets of eyes stared at him.

Two pairs of small arms clung to his thighs.

Lindy stood there, her mouth open.

DJ spun around to head back up the stairs.

"Sit down!" Robert's words snapped DJ around like a whip. She parked herself on the bottom step, but when she tried to lean back as if she didn't care what he said, her body wouldn't lean. Instead, her arms wrapped around her knees, and she hid her face in the comfort of her worn jeans.

She heard the soft *woosh* of air from the pillows of the sofa as someone sank into it. Her mother was following Robert's instructions, too. The boys sniffled, followed by another *woosh* from the sofa. Robert this time? She peeked beyond the safety of her arms. Robert now had one arm around her mother, but Lindy was sitting as stiffly as her daughter. The boys had divided, one sticking with Robert, the other with Lindy.

Only DJ was alone.

The carpet from the stairs to the sofa looked about five hundred miles wide.

She shut her eyes against the sight and ordered herself not to cry. *Don't you dare!* She wanted to plug her ears against the voice that whispered inside her head, *It was your fault, you know*.

What would Gran say when she heard about this latest mess?

"Now, I know we're all uptight, what with the wedding coming and the storm, but fighting isn't going to solve anything. It never does." Robert's voice was firm.

Maybe not, but it makes me feel better, DJ argued.

Yeah, right, it does.

Her nose itched, and she needed a tissue. Her throat filled, and her eyes burned. *I'm not going to cry*. DJ's nose began to drip.

God, you know I hate it when I get mad like this. I might as well have beat those two little guys up like I wanted to.

Look at them. DJ sneeked another peek. Her mother looked like someone had sucker-punched her, her face was so white and pinched, and there were black blotches under her eyes. Was she tired, or had her mascara smeared?

Lindy rubbed both her eyes and her forehead. "I agree. This family has to learn to talk out problems without getting into a fight."

But we're not *a family—not yet!*

DJ could hear footsteps coming closer. One sniff, then another, told her it was the Double Bs.

A small hand came to rest on her arm. "DJ, please. We's sorry."

Another hung on her other arm. "Please, DJ? We won't ever touch your stuff again. Ever. We promise."

Much against her will, DJ wrapped an arm around each of them. "I'm sorry, too, guys. I shoulda been watching you like I was supposed to."

"You should have put your things away, too. This wouldn't have happened then," Lindy said, her voice as tired as her face.

Instead of answering her mother, DJ hugged the boys. *As usual, everything is my fault*.

"Look, I'm sorry I'm not perfect like—" One look at Robert's face and DJ snapped her mouth shut. She waited again. "Mom, Robert, I'm sorry. Please forgive me?"

When Robert nodded and smiled at her, she looked to the boys, who stood, sober as sticks, by her knees. "You too?"

They threw their arms around her neck. "We love you, DJ."

"I love you guys, too." She squeezed them back, feeling the anger drain right out of her head and down and out through her toes. She took in a deep breath. "Don't worry, guys, I'll draw the pictures again. Fiddle, maybe they'll come out even better the second time. Besides, you didn't ruin them all."

But later, after Robert and the boys had left, DJ realized her mother hadn't said she'd forgiven her yet. In fact, she hadn't said anything to DJ since. What was going on now?

Should I go in and talk to Mom, or should I wait for her to come to me? Maybe I should just skip the whole thing. DJ chose the latter and, after gathering up her things for the morning and cleaning up the mess the boys had left, climbed into bed and prayed. She snuggled down to get warm. How come Gran hadn't called to say Joe was home? How come DJ's life was always such a disaster?

A note on the message board greeted her in the morning. *Please forgive me, DJ. I was too tired to think last night. I forgave you immediately and didn't realize I hadn't said anything until much later. Tell Gran to call me at the office after one. I have a few things to take care of. Love, Mom.*

DJ read the words again. Now her heart felt just like the sun bursting through the clouds. A new day had come. She called Gran before running out the door, and Joe answered.

"Hi, kid. Sorry we didn't call last night, but it got to be so late."

"Are you okay?" DJ wrapped the cord around her finger.

"Other than feeling like I was run over by a fleet of eighteen-wheelers, I'll make it. That sandbag stuff is for younger guys. Look, I'll take care of the horses today if you'll do it tomorrow. I'm going back up with the guys to help clean up now that the river is down again."

"You want some help?"

"Sure, if your mom doesn't mind. They can use every able pair of hands we can get."

"I'll ask around the Academy today to see if others want to come."

DJ heard a horn honk. "My ride's here. See ya tonight."

By the end of the day, DJ had rounded up seven kids to help with the cleanup. They agreed to meet at the school at 8:00 A.M. on Sunday, bringing lunches and drinks for themselves. DJ reminded everyone to bring gloves and rain gear in case another storm struck.

"My dad can take a bunch in the van," Tony Andrada offered. "I'll ask him and call you if it doesn't work out."

When they drove up to the front of the school in the morning, the group had grown. Whole families were there besides the high school kids. Joe had everyone assigned a ride and the troop on the road within half an hour.

"Boy, you sure know how to get a group going." DJ looked at him with pride.

"They teach you crowd control at the police academy." Joe, driving the lead car, checked the rearview mirror. "Anyway, it was you who started the thing rolling. Any time I want something done from now on, I know who to call."

"DJ's always been one to fight for the underdog," Gran said. "I know Robert and Lindy would be here, too, if there wasn't so much to do before the wedding and so little time to do it in. Of course, losing part of the roof to that new addition sure didn't help anything."

"Yeah, now we're going to have to live in our cramped

house longer." DJ shook her head. "How can two five-year-old boys take up so much room? They aren't very big."

"Boys always take up more room than girls," Hilary said from the seat next to DJ. "Our house felt empty when my big brother went off to college."

DJ couldn't believe her eyes when they drove up Highway 29. Half of the vineyards were still underwater, the knobby grape vines looking like grotesque arms reaching above the water's surface.

Joe talked on his cell phone for a few minutes, then directed the caravan into a housing development that bordered the Napa River. Mud covered everything, filling the streets and yards. The flood's high-water mark had crept two feet up on the walls of the houses.

"Pee-uw." DJ wanted to hold her nose. "How come floods smell so bad?"

"Well, the sewer lines and septic tanks were flooded, for one thing, plus some barnyards and—"

"I get the picture." DJ looked longingly at the many boxes of food in the back of the Explorer. "You guys must have been making sandwiches all night."

"Close. You watch, though, they'll disappear fast."

A man with a Day-Glo orange vest came to the door before they could climb out. "Hi, Joe, see ya brought the troops."

"Sure did. How you want them deployed?"

Frank Smith introduced himself, then gave everyone instructions and handed out shovels and rakes to the empty-handed. They all set to work, some inside the houses, and some out. DJ helped tear up carpets, scrape away mud, scrub inside and outside walls, and rake the worst of the mess off people's yards. Soon, a huge, brown worm of dirt grew in the middle of the street, waiting for the loaders and trucks to haul it away.

Gran carried the boxes of food and bottles of water and

soda to one spot, and Frank announced that homeowners were welcome to come help themselves. The food disappeared as Joe had promised. Shoveling mud was mighty hungry work.

"My arms are killing me," DJ moaned to Hilary. The two of them and John Yamamoto had been a team all day.

John shook his head. "I'm sure glad we live on a hill. Mom has always wanted to live near a river, but there's not a chance she'll get her way now."

"I've got aches where I didn't know I had muscles." Hilary dumped another scoop into the wheelbarrow. "At least we get to go home to hot showers. All these people can't." She gestured at the houses around them. "Those that have water have to boil it before they can use it."

DJ looked down at her clothes, caked solid with mud. "For once, my mom will be right when she says I stink!"

Instead of going shopping that night, DJ fell asleep in the bathtub. She'd taken a shower first to wash the mud off, then soaked her aching muscles. Her mother helped her into bed.

"What a mess," DJ mumbled as she drifted off to sleep.

At school Monday, DJ wasn't the only one walking like a frozen zombie. Others who'd helped wore the same half-open eyes and winced whenever they sat down or stood up. It was especially difficult to keep her eyes open during the film in history.

"DJ." The gentle voice and the tap on the shoulder seemed to come from far away.

"Huh?" Her cheek felt smashed, and her eyes hot.

"DJ, I think you should wake up now. The bell is about to ring." Ms. Fisher smiled down at her.

DJ felt like crawling under the desk or melting into a puddle and sliming out the door. How long had she been asleep?

"Way to go." The boy in the desk behind her poked her in the back.

The bell rang, and the race for the door was on.

DJ couldn't look the teacher or anyone else in the eye. She'd never fallen asleep in class before. What would her mother say? Surely one time wasn't concern enough for the teacher to send a note home with her.

"DJ." Ms. Fisher called her name.

"Yes?" DJ studied the tip of her fingernail.

"Don't feel so bad. I thought the movie was boring, too. Besides, I heard what you did yesterday. From what the other teachers have been saying, you're not the only one who's fallen asleep in class today."

"Thanks, but I still feel like an idiot."

"Just get some extra rest tonight. Good thing there are people like you in this world who care about others. I'm proud of you."

It was amazing how awake DJ felt after the compliment—even algebra went well.

At the Academy, she worked with Patches for her usual hour, carefully keeping to the outer edge of the ring. The jumps had been set up again, and Mrs. Ellsindorf had enlisted one of the stable hands to manage the standards and bars for her. DJ wanted to watch but knew that taking her attention off Patches would be a mistake.

"I should have put you out on the hot walker," she muttered after another session of crow-hopping. Patches flicked his ear back and forth, taking in the action in the middle of the ring, the conversations at the barns, and anything else going on within eye or earshot.

"Give it up!" The mischievous horse had rounded his spine and tried to get his head down for the umpteenth time.

DJ forced him to stand for a full three minutes until he finally let out his breath. From then on, he behaved perfectly.

"Patches, you old clown, what is your family going to do with you? What will it take for you to behave all the time, not just when you are ready?" He kept the steady lope in his line three feet from the walls and rails.

"You handle him so well," Mrs. Johnson said with a smile. "It's a pleasure to watch you two."

"How long have you been standing there?"

"Not long."

Good, then she didn't see her horse acting like a bronco. "When will you be starting your lessons with me?"

"Whenever you say. I'm ready anytime now." Mrs. Johnson reached over the bar to rub Patches' neck. "I know all I have to do is learn to make him mind me." She looked up at DJ. "And I'm counting on you to show me how. You're doing so well with Andrew that I know we'll do fine, too."

DJ felt a warm spot in her middle at the compliments. "Andrew is the one who's working hard, you know."

"I know. Say, I'll take Patches back and put him away, if you like. I know you have a lesson coming up with Bridget." She swung open the gate, giving a merry wave to Mrs. Ellsindorf at the same time.

Patches shot straight up in the air.

11

"KNOCK IT OFF, PATCHES." DJ threw her weight forward and smacked the rearing horse between the ears.

Patches dropped to his feet and shook his head.

"DJ, I'm so sorry! That was all my fault." Mrs. Johnson had the fence rails in a death grip.

"No problem. Wait here. We'll be right back." DJ signaled the horse to a jog and took him around the arena, calling him every kind of name she could think of. Patches never even flicked an ear, his head low. If a horse could be embarrassed, he certainly acted that way.

"You are the greatest actor I ever met." DJ's voice had gone from scolding to teasing. She stopped him back at the gate.

"Is he all right?" Mrs. Johnson swung the gate open very carefully.

"Patches looks for things to spook at. In fact, you should have named him Spook." DJ swung off the horse and walked beside his owner. "You just have to watch him every single moment. Lots of horses settle down more as they get older." She rubbed Patches' nose. "I'm sure he will, too."

DJ hoped and prayed she was right. Otherwise, how

could the Johnson family ever go trail-riding together like they wanted?

After the pounding Patches had given her, riding Megs for her own lesson felt like sitting on a padded cushion. DJ concentrated on every aspect of her body position and movement, as well as that of her horse, keeping Megs on the bit and bending around the leg like Jackie had taught her. When Bridget signaled her to the side to talk, DJ actually looked forward to it.

"You did well, *ma petite*."

"Merci."

Bridget smiled up at her. "You are learning quickly. Now to transfer that learning to Major."

"I know. At least I know what 'right' feels like now. I can see what you mean about both horse and rider becoming better athletes through dressage."

"Riding Lord Byron did not make you want to concentrate on dressage?"

On Saturday, DJ had told Bridget all about her fantastic rides. DJ shook her head. "There's just nothing like being airborne. Even Lord Byron didn't leave the ground."

"Spoken like a true jumper. Ah, well, we have plenty of work ahead. Next week, you should be able to work with Major again. Do not rush him, though. Build up the strength in that leg slowly so it does not become a recurring problem."

"I will." DJ thought a moment. "How slowly do you mean?"

"A very wise question." Bridget laid out a plan for the next two weeks, patted Megs on the shoulder, and turned to answer a request from another rider.

After putting Megs away, DJ fed Major, Ranger, and

Josh, scooped out some droppings, and jumped on her bike to head home. With Joe working on cleanup at home and Amy still on the sick list, she felt as if a chunk of her world was missing. She wished she dared stop by Amy's, but a phone call would have to do. Her mother might already be home, and tonight they were finally going to pick up the wedding dresses and shop for something for DJ to wear at the horse show.

"Mom, I'm home," DJ yelled up the stairs, hearing the sound of running water. When there was no answer, she took the steps two at a time and tapped on the door to her mother's bathroom. "I'm home," she repeated.

"Good. Can you be ready to leave in half an hour?" Lindy called back.

"I'll hurry."

She made it in twenty-nine minutes flat.

"The dresses are beautiful," Gran said later at the restaurant. "I'm glad I didn't try to make them myself."

"You would have made them beautifully, too." Lindy looked up from reading her menu.

"Oh, I know, but they wouldn't have been ready by now, and my book illustrations wouldn't have been done for my deadline, either."

"And you'd have been a basket case." Lindy smiled. "Let alone me. Things are bad enough as they are."

"Bad how?" DJ asked.

"Bad as in so crazy I can't keep up." Lindy raised her hands palm up. "You know, this is the first time in weeks I haven't had somewhere else I had to be or something to do as soon as I get home."

"So everything is set for the wedding, then."

"Out of the mouths of babes." Gran's eyes held a twinkle

that said she wholeheartedly agreed.

"Not that I'm a babe."

"No, not a babe of either kind," Lindy said. "And thank God, too."

DJ looked from her mother to her grandmother, then broke out in laughter. Her mother had tickled her funny bone.

"I don't see what's so funny." Lindy looked puzzled.

Gran shrugged and shook her head. The twinkle in her eyes said *she* got the joke.

So her mother hadn't meant to be funny. DJ took a long swallow from her soda. Oh well, at least she knew her mother had a sense of humor somewhere in there, even though she claimed she couldn't remember the punch line of a joke if she were paid to.

Somehow they managed to find just the right clothes for DJ—and without her having to try on fifty different things, which she disliked doing even more than algebra. The navy bomber jacket looked good with tan pants, jeans, or even a skirt—if DJ had owned one. With a couple of new turtlenecks and a V-neck sweater, along with some clothes she already owned, DJ could mix and match to go anywhere.

When her mother insisted on buying her some chunky-heeled dress boots, DJ didn't argue. A small purse with a long, thin shoulder strap would take the place of her back-pack.

"Thanks, Mom, Gran," DJ said for the umpteenth time.

"You're welcome." Lindy looked up in the rearview mirror to catch DJ's eye. "I still think we should have gotten you the robe and pj's."

"I don't need them."

"Sure you do. In fact, I think I'll pick them up after work tomorrow. Do have enough underwear?"

"M-o-t-h-e-r."

"She's not going to the moon and back," Gran said with a chuckle. When Lindy started to say something, Gran continued. "This just shows you are really a mother at heart after all, dear. I wonder how many times I told you to be sure to have clean underwear—no holes—"

"Just in case I had an accident and had to go to the emergency room," Lindy and DJ finished the words together.

The warm glow remained inside DJ's heart as she put her new things away and got ready for bed. Shopping hadn't been so bad after all.

"Thanks, God, today was super. And thanks that Amy gets to come back to school tomorrow—I've sure missed her. Please help all the people who've been flooded and thanks for keeping Joe safe, as well as Brad and Jackie and all their horses." She fell asleep still giving thanks.

DJ and Amy talked nonstop on the way to school in the morning, through lunch, and on the way home. They still hadn't gotten caught up when it was time to leave for the Academy. Since the sun and clouds were in a contest for first place, they rode their bikes for a change, but pumping up the hill set Amy to coughing.

"You sure you shouldn't go home and rest? I can take care of Josh another day or two." DJ paused to wait until Amy caught her breath.

"No way! I've been in jail too long already. I was about

to call you to come bust me out." The talking made her cough again. "This will go away some year—the doctor said so."

"Okay, but—"

"No buts. Get your legs moving, we've got horses waiting for us!"

That night, Brad called to tell her that Jackie had left that morning with Lord Byron and a friend's horse in the trailer. The two women were driving and wanted to get to the showgrounds a couple of days early to get acclimated.

"You and I will be flying. We have an early flight on Friday out of San Francisco, so how about if I pick you up Thursday evening about six or six-thirty? Traffic should have let up by then."

DJ felt a shiver run up her back. She was finally going to see what a top-level dressage show was like! " 'Kay. I'll be ready. See ya."

When the phone rang again, it was Robert. DJ expected the call to be for her mother, but he said he wanted to speak with her first.

"What's up?" DJ leaned against the counter, one elbow propped on the top.

"How about you and I go out to dinner tomorrow night and then by the house? I have some questions about how you want your room done."

"Done?"

"You know—colors, carpet, things like that. We can put in bookshelves, too, so you have storage space for your art supplies."

"Oh."

"That okay?"

"Ah . . . sure. What time?" *But what do I know about*

decorating a room? It would help if she didn't sound like a yo-yo brain when they talked.

They finished making their plans with Robert saying he'd set it up with her mother.

DJ snagged a can of soda from the fridge, dug in the drawer for an apple, bumped the door shut with her foot, then wandered upstairs to her room. She stared at the posters of horses on her walls—horses jumping, playing, racing; mares and foals in the field; horses in stalls. A large picture of Major held the place of honor. Her own drawings took up lots of space, too. But it was the intertwined Olympic rings over the head of a bay horse, front feet tucked close to his chest as he cleared a brick wall, that brought her to a stop. Only on television had she seen horses and riders of this caliber. Maybe one day Brad would take her to one of the big jumping shows. She might see one of *her* heroes there.

Visions of her jumping with a horse that looked surprisingly like Lord Byron sent her off to sleep.

"So where would you like to go for dinner?" Robert asked once they were in the car.

DJ started to say, "I don't know," then stopped herself. "What would *you* like?"

"Not pizza."

DJ agreed. That was the Bs favorite meal in all the world, besides fried chicken and hamburgers. "You want ribs?"

"Not tonight. Chinese?"

DJ thought a moment. She always liked Chinese food. "Honey-walnut prawns?"

"You've got it. You want to choose which restaurant?"

"The one down on Contra Costa, across from Taco

Bell." DJ fastened her seat belt. "We haven't been there in a long time."

While they were waiting for their dinner to be served, Robert opened a folder and laid some fabric, paint, and carpet samples on the table. "Have you been thinking of what you'd like in your room?"

"Honest, I'm clueless."

"Okay, I'll ask questions, and you answer." At her nod, he began. "Entertainment center?"

"For what?"

"Don't you have a television or stereo? What about a VCR?" When she shook her head at all of the above, he stared at her. "I thought all teenagers had those things."

"Not this one. I have a small boom box, but it's broken. I use the one downstairs."

At his puzzled look, she drew in a breath. "I know I'm strange, but I like it quiet when I study and even more so when I draw. I get so lost in what I'm doing, I don't need noise."

"Well, you've relieved my mind on one account, that's for sure." He grinned at her questioning look. "I was afraid my hearing would go due to loud music."

"Not mine."

"Do you have any books?"

"Mostly on horses and drawing, but I do have some novels, too."

"Computer?"

"I wish."

Their food came, but Robert kept on asking questions while they ate. "What about storage for your art supplies and a drafting table?"

"Really?"

"Sure. We'll include shelves and drawers for a computer in your work area, too, since I think you should have one."

"Have you talked with Mom about all this?"

"No. Why?" He stopped with a prawn halfway to his mouth. "It's your room."

When she just stared at him, he set down his chopsticks. "What? Do I have some sauce on my chin?"

She shook her head. "I think I better pinch myself to see if I'm dreaming."

"I thought maybe we should tile the area around the drafting table so you can put an easel there if you'd like, too. Gran suggested that. She said that someday you might do more than pencil drawings. You'll have a place to work at her home as well because she's going to add studio space when they rebuild the garage."

"She is?" DJ got the feeling they'd been doing a lot of talking without her knowledge.

"Yes, they'll be adding a potter's wheel and kiln then, too. Gran thought that would be something all the grandchildren could enjoy." He smiled again. "You want that last prawn?"

When DJ shook her head, he popped it in his mouth, along with the last walnut. "They can box the leftovers."

"What leftovers?" DJ teased.

Once at the new house, DJ and Robert made their way upstairs to the original master bedroom, which was slotted to become DJ's new room.

"I thought maybe we'd add a window over here—floor length, if you like—and this area would work for your art supplies and desk. What do you think?"

Walking in front of her, he pointed to the closet. "We'll put all the space-saving goodies in there—you know, shelves, drawers, and that kind of thing, And then," he indicated an entire wall, "this would look great done in floor-to-ceiling shelves for books and art and trophies."

Dazed, DJ followed Robert into the large bathroom. "We can do both a shower and a tub in here, if you want. I thought maybe you'd like a tub with jets to help work out your sore muscles. Lindy says the hot tub outside will be enough but—"

"Whoa, Robert!" DJ held up a hand. "If we were talking about a barn, I would have good ideas about what to do, but this . . . this is kinda much. I like everything you've suggested. How can I choose?"

"DJ." He turned and rested a hand on her shoulder. "You don't have to choose one thing over another unless you want to. The basic structure is what's important right now, like the new window or adding more closet space. The new tub would have to go in now, too, of course. Gran said she'd help you pick out colors, but we could ask a decorator to pitch in if you'd rather." He stood back, waiting.

DJ sucked in a deep breath. "I'd love to have big windows, but the closet is fine. I'll leave it to you to decide on the tub. I'm a shower person unless my muscles are really yelling. Everything else sounds wonderful." She paused to sort through it all.

"I'm not sure what colors offhand." She thought hard. "Maybe different shades of blue, with sand and—"

"I get the picture. If we could find wood in a deep, blood bay shade, how would that be?"

"Perfect." She glanced up at him out of the corner of her eye. "I've always liked gray, too—as in dappled. And Lippizaner white can't be beat."

Robert clasped an arm around her shoulders. "You've got your head on straight, DJ, that's for sure. And when we get to building the barn, you can help draw up the blueprints."

DJ took one last look at the room before turning out the light. *Wait till Amy hears about this!*

They were nearly back to her house when Robert said,

"You know, I have a favor to ask."

"What?"

"Can you be extra patient with your mother in the next week or so? She's pretty uptight about the wedding and all."

"Who isn't?" The words just slipped out. "Sorry."

"I know, we all are. There's just so much to be done yet." He clicked on his turn signal. "I want all of us to be relaxed and ready to enjoy the wedding—no fights, no tempers. Maybe I'm dreaming, but I'm giving everyone this speech, including me. If we all cut each other some slack, we'll do all right."

"I'll try." DJ shook her head. "Cancel that. I'll do it."

Robert parked the car in the driveway and turned off thc lights. "I know you will."

When they got out, they had to run to the house to keep from getting wet. The rain had returned.

12

"THANKS, LINDY, FOR LETTING DJ come with us. I'll have her home early Sunday night."

"I appreciate that." Lindy turned to DJ. "Now, you call if there's any change of plans."

DJ nodded and gave her mother a hug. "See you." She tried to act nonchalant, but keeping the excitement down was like trying to stop the rain. She'd be flying to a big-time horse show in the morning!

Brad picked up her duffel bag and held the door open for her. Feeling like the queen bee herself, DJ headed for the Land Rover. The rain had changed from a light mist to a sheeting blanket.

The drive to the farm passed with the kind of conversation two people have who are devoted to the same pastime. Neither one could ever talk horses too much. The heavy rain made it impossible to see the water-covered lowlands of the Napa Valley, the Sonoma Valley, and then the Petaluma, but Brad told her about them all.

When they stepped out of the car, DJ could hear the river that flowed between the levees at the low end of the fields.

"Let's take your things in and get some rain gear, then I need to check that mare. You can come if you want."

"Sure I do. Do you think she'll foal tonight?"

"I hope not—but then I thought she would foal last week some time. You never can tell for sure."

Brad unlocked the door and motioned DJ inside. "I have a lantern down at the barn. I hate to turn on all the lights and wake the horses up." He carried her bag to her room. "There's plenty of rain gear by the door, so you needn't unpack yours. Jackie called today and said it's really nice down south. Wish some of that sun would make its way back up here."

DJ draped her wet Windbreaker over the chair and followed her father back down the hall. Thanks to the drumming rain, even the house felt damp. She rubbed her arms. Good thing she had a sweater on.

The rain sounded even louder on the roof of the horse barn. Brad flicked the switch on a battery-operated lantern hanging right inside the doorway, and a soft glow spread a circle around them. The lights from the Land Rover automatically shut off as Brad slid the barn door closed.

A horse nickered from somewhere in the dimness. Straw rustled under restless hooves. Both foaling stalls were occupied. In one the mare stood placidly in the corner, opening her eyes just enough to acknowledge the two humans before going back to dozing. In the other, the heavy-sided mare paced and rocked from one foot to another.

"Uh-oh." Brad handed DJ the lantern. He opened the stall door and motioned her to step inside with him.

From the books she'd read, DJ knew that restlessness could be an indication of beginning or first-stage labor in a mare.

The mare's tail twitched, and she reached past her shoulder to nip at her ribs, a sign of pain. She paced and shifted, then paced and shifted again.

"I'll be right back, old girl." Brad patted the mare one

more time and left the stall. "You ever wrapped a horse's tail?"

"For shows."

"This isn't much different—just not as fancy." Brad went to the tack room and returned with a roll of white wrap. "Here, I'll start and then you can do it. Set the lantern on the shelf there."

He wrapped the first couple of rounds, starting at the top of the tail, then handed DJ the roll. "Go most of the way down with this. It keeps her tail from tangling in the birth sac."

DJ tested the tightness and continued wrapping. "How many foals has she had?"

"Ten or so, I think. She's an old hand at it, anyway, so I don't expect any trouble." He repositioned the camera monitor in the corner so it could view the entire stall. "This way I can check on her without coming down to the barn. Stupid thing is, I let Ramone have the night off because he'll be here full time when we're down at the show." He stroked the mare's sweaty neck, talking to her in a soothing voice.

Watching him, DJ knew where she got her horse sense.

"Did you always love horses like this?" she asked softly.

"I've always liked them, but I think the love grew as I got older. My hope of owning a horse-breeding and showing ranch was just a dream for many years. I had to become established as an attorney first. Then I met Jackie at a horse show, and we put our dreams together." As he spoke, he walked around the mare, keeping a gentle hand on her at all times. He checked her udder. "Couldn't you wait a couple more days, old girl?"

She snorted, then bent her front legs and collapsed with a grunt on her side.

"Good. If you're going to do this, let's get it over with." Brad knelt beside her, continuing to stroke her neck.

The mare surged to her feet and began the rocking and pacing motion again. But within a few minutes, she quieted down, relaxed, and began to doze.

"Now what?"

"The contractions have stopped for who knows how long. Could be an hour, could be twenty-four. Some mares refuse to have their foal while a human is anywhere around, but I've been with Soda here for the last four, so I know that's not the case."

"I read once that wild horses could stop the birthing if danger threatened."

"Not just wild ones. That's why we set up the monitoring system. A thermostat keeps it the perfect temperature in here, too. Neither too cold nor too hot is good for the foal."

"I didn't know it could be so complicated."

"Yeah, well, when foals are worth thousands of dollars, you can't be too careful." Brad checked his watch. "It's nearly nine. Morning is going to come awfully early, so maybe you should hit the sack."

"And miss this?"

"No, you won't miss anything. I'll keep checking her, and if she goes into stage-two labor, I'll wake you."

"Promise?"

"Promise."

"If it comes on fast, I may miss it." DJ glanced over her shoulder at the mare, who now looked as if nothing had happened. She opened her eyes and exhaled a heavy breath as they left the large, loose box stall, but even her ears didn't twitch.

"You want anything to eat or drink?" Brad asked when they reached the kitchen. He pointed to the TV in the corner, which showed the mare sound asleep in her stall. "I'm having hot chocolate."

"That sounds good." DJ pulled out a bar stool and

turned so she could watch the screen.

"I have another screen in my bedroom. I can set it to wake me however often I want so I can check on her. Of course, it would be better to have a man down there at the barn, but I think we still have a couple of hours or more to go."

After finishing the cocoa, DJ headed for bed, certain she'd never go to sleep. She was not only going to a horse show in the morning, she was going to watch a foal come into the world! She whispered her thank-yous and blessings into the stillness of the dark room. Without streetlights like at home, the dark here was really dark, even with the blinds left wide open. "And please, God, take care of Soda and her baby."

A tree branch brushed against the window, startling DJ from the doze she was sure would never come. She took in a deep breath and pulled the covers up over her ears. Why had a dumb tree branch startled her?

"DJ," Brad's voice floated out of the darkness sometime later, "it looks like we're going to have a foal tonight." Her father touched her shoulder.

"Okay."

"I'll meet you in the kitchen." He left the room.

"Okay."

DJ blinked hard, trying to get her eyes to stay open as she hopped from the bed and into her clothes. She added a long-sleeved turtleneck under the sweat shirt and heavy socks to keep her feet warm inside her boots. Slicking her hair back and wrapping a scrunchie around it as she walked, she got to the kitchen as Brad hung up the phone.

"Ramone is on his way. He said the river is rising fast. Apparently, there was more rain to the north of us than we had here. They're sandbagging the levee upriver." He shook his head. "If the water overflows, we could be in a world of trouble."

"You think it could?"

"I doubt it, but stranger things have happened. For now, first things first. Soda doesn't look like she's waiting on us."

DJ glanced at the monitor screen. The mare was rising to her feet again.

The roar of the river was muted by the barn walls. Soda had lain down again but heaved herself back up when they entered the stall.

"Move very slowly around her from now on," Brad cautioned. "The calmer we are, the easier it will be for her." He circled the mare. "No sign of the sac yet. It might still be a while."

DJ stroked Soda's neck and smoothed her cheek. The mare seemed to accept her there, though her restlessness continued.

When the water broke, Brad breathed a sigh of relief. "Soon now."

Fifteen minutes passed.

To DJ, it seemed like two days. She listened as her father softly explained all that was happening with the mare and unborn foal.

"You want to interfere as little as possible," he said. "God set this process in motion, and it works better when you leave it alone—unless you're sure there's trouble. And I'm thinking more and more that's what we're in here."

"Are you going to call the vet?"

"Not yet, but it's a real possibility."

She and Brad both sat in a corner of the stall. Another ten minutes dragged by. The mare was down, then up, back down on one side, then the other.

"Something is definitely wrong. Now that she's up, I'm going to check to see if the foal is in the right position." He took off his jacket and pulled a long, sterile rubber glove from the bucket he'd brought from the tack room. "Hold her head for me, please."

DJ watched as he carefully inserted his hand into the birth canal. The mare flinched but stood still. "What is it?"

"I can't find the other foot." He reached farther. "It's bent back at the knee." A contraction clamped around his arm, making him wince.

"You okay?"

"Better than this baby here." He gritted his teeth. "I've got to get that leg straightened out. That's what's slowing her down." He closed his eyes as another contraction squeezed off the circulation all the way to his shoulder. "Okay, girl, now as you relax, let me find that hoof."

Please, God, help him. DJ kept on stroking the horse and pleading for help at the same time.

"Got it." He grunted again. "You have to be careful that you don't injure either the foal or the sac it's in. The mare, either, for that matter." Brad sighed with relief. "There."

DJ sent a thank-you heavenward as her father withdrew his hand. Pulling the glove off, he came to stand beside her. The mare groaned and lay back down.

"She's on the right side now. And that little one is ready to join us."

They both hunkered down at the rear of the mare. The protruding sac had grown in size.

"You should see the front hooves any minute now." He kept a steady hand on the mare's haunches. "Come on, girl, I don't want to have to pull it."

DJ bit her lip in delight. Two tiny hooves, still covered by the white sac, inched out. Another contraction, and she could see the knees. On the next, the foal's head, nose pressed to the legs, appeared.

"Okay, girl, keep it coming. Right now, DJ, is a crucial moment. Too long at this point, and the baby could have breathing problems because its cord is being pinched."

While his voice was soft and even, DJ could hear the concern. Never had she realized how many things could go wrong.

With a mighty contraction on the mare's part, the foal, still totally covered by the white sac, slipped out onto the straw.

And didn't move.

Brad knelt beside the still form, ripped the sack away from the foal's head, and with a clump of straw, wiped out the tiny nostrils. Still no movement.

"It's not breathing. DJ, call the vet." He motioned to the cell phone in a holder in the corner. He gave her the number to punch in, then pinched the foal's lower nostril closed and blew into the upper nostril.

DJ's fingers were shaking so hard, she could hardly dial. She watched her father breathe in and blow out in a steady rhythm. He stopped to compress the foal's ribs.

The phone rang in her ear. *Please, God, please*. An answering machine kicked on. "Dr. Benton is out on a call right now. Please leave your number, and as soon as he can, he will check for messages and return your call."

"I got an answering machine."

"Leave our number. He'll call from his mobile phone as soon as he's back in his truck."

DJ did as she was told. At that moment, the foal's ribs rose and fell—the most beautiful sight DJ had seen in her whole life. The baby was breathing! It would live now. She set the phone down.

The foal pulled back against Brad's grip and began thrashing its feet.

Brad cleaned the remainder of the sack away and stepped back. "Thank God for His mercies."

"I did . . . I do." DJ could feel tears burning behind her eyes. *Don't cry now*, she scolded herself.

"Pretty amazing, isn't it?" Brad draped an arm across her shoulders and squeezed her to him. "Nearly makes me cry every time I see it."

DJ sniffed. "Good, then I don't feel like such an idiot."

"Seeing a miracle in action should make anyone cry. We're not out of the woods with this one yet, but at least we're on the right path."

Brad took a thick towel out of the bucket. "You want to rub her down?"

"The mare?"

"No, the foal. Soda will be on her feet in a while to start pushing this one to get up and begin nursing."

Brad collected the sac when the afterbirth came and put them both in a plastic bag.

"Why do you keep those?"

"If there's a problem, much can be learned from this. For instance, if there's an infection, it could tell us what kind and if all the afterbirth is out—if it isn't, the mare could get an infection, too. Also, it tells us if there was any problem for the foal before birth, such as a rip in the membranes or poor circulation."

"Oh."

The phone beeped, and Brad answered it. "We have a filly here, but she's weak because she was a long time coming. I had to go in and straighten a front leg, and she couldn't start breathing without help. Yes, I think we'll be okay. I'll let you know if things change."

But while the baby tried, an hour later she still didn't have her feet under her. Even DJ could tell the foal was getting tired.

Soda whuffled to her foal, licking her and pushing

sometimes with her nose. But the foal lay quietly after another major effort to stand.

"Look, Soda is dripping milk."

"She's losing her colostrum. We might have to tube-feed this one, so I'd better see if we can save some of that." Brad brought a plastic jar back from the tack room. "I have some frozen from another mare if we need it."

He said it so matter-of-factly that DJ nearly missed the point. The filly might not be able to nurse—and if it didn't eat, it would die. Her stomach clenched as though someone had tied a rope around it and jerked.

The sound of an automobile outside the barn captured their attention.

"Good, Ramone is here. He's a better milker than I am."

"Sorry I took so long. One road was flooded, so I had to go back around." Ramone took in the situation at a glance. "Trouble, eh?"

"Could you do the honors?" Brad handed him the jar. "Don't take too much in case she makes it up on her own and can nurse."

Brad took a clipboard off a nail and checked his watch, where he'd clicked the stop button when the foal fully emerged. "Born at 3:15, needed assistance with . . ." he mumbled as he wrote, then looked down at DJ, who sat in the corner watching the mare and foal. "Keep praying."

"I am."

He clicked another button on his watch. "Uh-oh. We should be leaving for the airport right about now."

Ramone broke in. "Like I said, the main road's closed. You should have left earlier." He capped the jar and set it on the shelf. "Sorry I got here so late."

"It wouldn't have made any difference. I wouldn't have left. We'll just have to take a later flight."

Relief made DJ's shoulders slump. She didn't want to

leave the foal right now, no matter how much she wanted to see Jackie compete.

By daylight, even with help, the foal had neither stood on her own nor been able to nurse. Brad called the vet again.

13

"HOW ABOUT IF I TRAILER a load of the horses up to the Carsons?"

Brad looked up at his foreman. "Something telling you that's what we should be doing?"

Ramone nodded. "Juan and I can do that. I really think we should get them all out of here." He took off his hat and scrubbed his dark hair smooth before putting it back on. "I've never seen the river so high—not since they built the levee. You always say it's better to be safe than sorry."

"It would take a Noah-type flood to reach the house."

"Sure, but the barns aren't up that high."

DJ watched the conversation ping-pong back and forth. Brad had insisted they come up to the house to eat. While she was hungry enough to devour the scrambled eggs he made, all she could think of was the foal. She had to stand and suck to nurse. Nothing major, unless she was too weak already.

A thought made her catch her breath. She choked on the toast in her mouth.

"You all right?" Brad leaned toward her.

DJ waved him away, then coughed, choked, and coughed again. A glass of water appeared in front of her.

She took a clear breath, swallowed a couple of gulps, and breathed deeply.

"I'm fine. Guess it went down the wrong spout." She could feel the heat in her face from both the coughing fit and embarrassment. She looked at her father. "You don't think something is wrong with the foal's lungs or anything, do you?"

"The thought's crossed my mind. This one seems to have had a couple of strikes against her before she even got here." He folded his arms on the table and leaned toward her. "DJ, sometimes these things happen. Maybe her lungs didn't develop quite right, or her heart. If that's the case, then the biggest favor we can do for her is put her down. We can't let her suffer."

DJ could feel the tears welling as fast as Brad was talking. *Put her down before she even has a chance to live? That's not fair! You've got to give her a chance*. She didn't dare say a word because then her tears would stream like the rain on the windows.

A car horn honked.

"Benton's here," Ramone said, checking out the window by the front door.

Brad looked over at DJ. "We'll know more after the vet examines her. Then we'll feed her using a stomach tube to see if that helps get her on her feet. I'll give her every chance, Deej. She's worth the time and effort."

The new nickname made DJ smile as she slid her arms into the brown jacket her father had loaned her. *Deej, huh?*

Back in the barn, nothing had changed. The mare hadn't given up on encouraging her foal, but the little one still lay flat out in the straw. DJ took a moment to thank God the foal was still breathing as she watched the vet, who, after donning a coverall and boots that had been rinsed in disinfectant, knelt beside the foal. He listened to her heart and lungs, belly sounds, then looked up the nostrils and in her mouth, eyes, and ears.

"Everything sounds normal," he said, rising to his feet. "She's just weak. Let's get some milk in her via the tube and see if that doesn't help. We should get her nursing on a false teat until she can stand on her own."

"False teat?" DJ looked to her father.

"A special nipple on a bottle that acts more like the real thing. Could you halter the mare and tie her to that bar, please?"

DJ did as he asked. In the meantime, Brad retrieved the milk from the refrigerator in the tack room and, after warming it in the microwave, returned to the stall.

By then, Dr. Benton had worked the rubber tubing up through the foal's nose and down its throat. Ramone held her while Brad slowly poured the colostrum into the cupped end of the tube.

"I'm going to take a blood sample to see if we're fighting any infections," the vet said as he located a vein in the foal's neck and pulled a syringe full of dark fluid. "Let her be for a while, then assist her once she struggles to her feet." He smiled at DJ. "Brad knows all of this, but repeating it never hurts, and I knew you'd want to know what's going on."

"Thanks." DJ left off stroking the mare and sank down behind the foal. She smoothed the fuzzy mane and brushed straw from the now dry coat. The foal raised her head and tried gathering her legs under her to be more upright. DJ inched closer to let the foal use her knees as a brace. With her legs folded under her, the baby rested her nose on the straw, still breathing heavily from the exertion.

Brad untied the mare but held the end of the rope. "She doesn't seem to mind you at all." The mare sniffed DJ's hair, then nudged her baby.

"Give her a minute, girl," DJ whispered.

"I've got another call to make," Dr. Benton said. "Call me if there's any change for the worse. Keep up the good work, DJ. I can tell you get along with horses like your dad does."

But an hour later, no matter how much DJ and the mare coaxed the foal, she could not get to her feet. DJ could hear the men loading horses into the long trailer outside. Matadorian was the first, followed by the better blooded show horses, until they had ten loaded. She heard the truck drive off, and Brad returned to the stall.

"DJ, I've set our tickets for the six o'clock flight. That means we need to leave here by three."

"You mean leave her like this?"

"Juan will take care of her. He's great with the foals."

"But . . . but I can't just leave her."

The mare nickered at the rise in DJ's voice and shifted from one foot to another.

DJ tried to calm down and forced her voice to a lower note. "Please."

"You've been up most of the night. Will you want to shower before we go?" Brad shrugged at the pleading look on her face. "What can I say, Deej? Jackie needs me with her, and the farm needs me here. The reality is sometimes I have to be gone—that's why I hire extremely capable people."

Ramone slid open the door and, trying to keep his voice low, stammered, "Bad news. The levee broke less than a mile upriver. Water is pouring into our side of the valley."

"I see. Well, there go our lower fields, but the water shouldn't pose a problem up this far. The house and barns will be fine."

"But if you don't leave right now, the road will be closed."

"I can't leave with something like this going on. Besides, that would leave you all alone. Juan won't be able to return with the truck." He turned back to the foaling stall. "Well, DJ, you got your wish. We aren't going anywhere." He closed his eyes. "Oh no. I better get you out of here. Your mother will have that proverbial cow for certain if she hears you're caught in a flood."

"No way—I'm not leaving." DJ got to her feet, nearly collapsing on the foot that had gone to sleep.

The mare laid her ears back. The foal struggled to rise, too, her thin legs scrambling but refusing to work together. She collapsed again, flat out, flanks heaving.

"Sorry to pull rank, but you have to go. And it has to be *now*, so I can get back."

"Where will you take her?" Ramone asked.

"To . . . ah, to the Lodesly place. I'll call them now. Her mother can pick her up there." He dialed but when the answering machine came on, he hit the cancel button. Another call had the same result.

DJ stood with her arms crossed, trying to keep the fury inside. He needed her here and instead he was trying to find someone else to keep her. He was right that Mom would be mad, but it wasn't as if they had planned this. "Mom will understand this was an emergency."

Brad handed her the phone. "The others have probably either left or are outside trying to salvage things from the flood. Their homes are on hills like this one, so their houses should be safe. At this point, it looks like we have no choice but for you to stay."

"Do you want me to call my mother?"

"Oh." Brad reached for the phone. "I'll do it." But when he dialed, the answering machine clicked on there, too. As he left a message, DJ shook her head.

"She's at work. Why not wait and tell her later when I can talk with her?"

"Too late, I've left the message." Brad pressed the off button again.

Suddenly, the barn turned dark as the dim barn lights flickered out. Rain-streaked windows let in what little outdoor light remained.

"We've got to keep it warm enough for the foal in here, so let's get the generator going. Ramone, you start that, and I'll go up to the house and turn off the switches. DJ, why don't you call your grandmother so she doesn't worry."

"Okay."

This time when the phone rang, there was someone to pick it up.

"DJ, are you all right?" Gran's voice carried the love of years through the wire.

"We're fine, Gran, but we haven't left for Los Angeles yet—or rather now we won't."

"What's happening?"

"Well, the mare foaled during the night, and the baby has some problems, so we've been working with her. And we just got word that the levee broke and . . . no, Gran, we'll be okay. Brad says the house and barns are high enough on the hill that we're in no danger—we're just stuck here. No, by the time you could get here, the roads will be flooded. Don't worry, I'm safe." She almost mentioned them relocating some of the horses, but she thought the better of it. "Oh, and, Gran, please pray for this filly. She just hasn't got the strength to stand, and if she can't stand, she can't nurse. I'll be feeding her from the bottle."

After promising to keep them posted and saying goodbye, DJ set the phone back in its cradle. Now if only she could get the foal to stand.

One of the Bible verses Gran had given DJ when she wanted to quit chewing her fingernails came floating through her mind. *Not by might nor by power, but by my Spirit, says the Lord*. She hummed the tune it was set to as she approached the stall again.

The mare turned from pulling hay out of the sling and pricked her ears. DJ heard a chugging sound, and the lights flickered and came back on.

"See, that's what God means about His Spirit," she confided to the mare. "With His Spirit, there is light and heat. God's power is stronger than even that crazy river." The more DJ said the words, the more she believed them herself. They were safe from the flood, but what about the weak foal? Surely God meant for His Spirit to take care of all His living creatures.

DJ let herself back into the stall and eased next to the mare, stroking her neck and watching the foal sleep. "God, you've brought us this far. Thanks for that. Now please give this filly the strength to stand and nurse so she can grow right and healthy. She is so little and weak." DJ sniffed and wished she had a handkerchief. "Please help us again."

She leaned against the mare, inhaling the scent of horse. She could hear the mare in the next stall, groaning as she lay down. Was she going into labor, too? Down the aisle, the remaining horses ate or dozed, the contented sounds of a normal barn. From outside, she could hear the river.

The door squeaked open, and Ramone entered, followed by Brad.

"You can see the river," Ramone was saying.

"I know, but it won't climb this high." Brad leaned over the stall and handed DJ a zipped plastic bag. "You might want to wash your hands first, but I figured if you were as hungry as I am, your stomach rumbling might scare the old girl here." He nodded toward the mare.

"Thanks." DJ grinned and slumped down the stall wall, crossing her legs to sit more comfortably. Rubbing her hands mostly clean on her thighs, she pulled half the sandwich from the bag and attacked.

"We could go sit on the chairs in my office—I have the coffee machine on, and I know there are sodas in the refrigerator."

"I'm fine. How long before we feed her again?"

"Any time Ramone wants to milk the mare. I have powdered substitute to mix, too, but the more colostrum we can get in her, the better."

"Did you check on the fields?" DJ looked up to see Ramone standing beside her father.

"I did. I just hope there's plenty of good fertilizer in that mud because it will be a while before our grass can push up through it."

"It's only mud?" DJ asked around a bite of ham and cheese.

"Nope, there's a lot of water, too. You can actually watch it rising up the slope. I sure am glad I didn't put the buildings down on the flat when we built. Was tempted to at the time."

Suddenly, the roar of helicopter blades seemed to hang right over the barn. "The river has flooded, and the water will continue to rise," the voice echoed above. "Please evacuate. If you need help, wave something white."

Brad went out in the driving rain and waved them off. Even though the sound of the blades disappeared, the rain drumming on the roof and cascading through the downspouts made enough noise to make talking softly difficult.

DJ could feel herself slipping into her own world, a place where the sun shone and foals danced across a fenced pasture. A place where Major rolled in knee-deep grass and then took her jumping over the fences. She fought to keep her eyes open.

Ramone entered the stall. "Would you please hold Soda while I see if I can get some more milk for the little one?"

"Sure." DJ yawned when she stood up to take hold of Soda, who twitched her tail and shifted her front feet, but standing still for the most part. "Will you put a tube down the filly again?"

"No, this time we'll use the bottle. You'll do well with her, I know."

When Ramone returned, he had the artificial teat connected to a squarish plastic bottle. "Just see if you can get her to suck on it. She'll probably fight you if you try to open her jaws, but she'll get the hang of it eventually."

DJ looked from the bottle to the foal. Why did this seem like it could be difficult? Surely the baby was hungry enough now to take about anything.

But it didn't work that way. When DJ held the nipple against the foal's lips, she shook her head. Then DJ held the baby's head and tried to force the nipple in, but the struggle wasn't worth it. As the foal fought DJ, the mare grew more restless, finally laying her ears back.

"Don't worry about Soda. She's tied up." Ramone lowered himself down beside DJ. "Try wetting your fingers with the milk and rubbing it on her lips."

DJ did, but the foal would have none of it.

Once more she tried, this time by pressing down on the lower jawbone and inserting the nipple from the side. Nada.

Pleading, coaxing, dribbling the milk in the cup of the lower lip—nothing worked. Only her jeans grew wet from all the milk that bypassed the baby's throat.

"She's stubborn, that one." Brad returned from making some more phone calls. "Why don't you call it a day? You look about done in."

"What are you going to do?"

"Ramone and I are going to move the equipment out of the office and the tack room and store it all upstairs. Just in case."

"Just in case what?"

"Just in case the water does indeed get up to the barn.

I didn't think it could happen but . . ."

DJ went to stand at the door. Sure enough. It looked like the house and barns were on an island surrounded by dirty brown water all the way around—and coming closer.

14

"HAVE YOU EVER FILLED SANDBAGS?" Brad asked in a teasing tone.

DJ noticed the smile never quite reached his eyes. "No, but I did clean up a flood site last weekend over in Napa."

"Well, let's hope and pray it doesn't come to that." Brad turned back to Ramone. "But better safe than sorry, right?"

Ramone fingered his gray-flecked mustache. "We'd better get started—we have a lot of doors in this barn. And we'd better begin with the well house."

"You're right. If that generator gets flooded, we won't have any clean water. Boiling water for this many horses will be almost impossible." Brad visibly relaxed his shoulders.

A jingle played in DJ's head. *Water, water, everywhere—and not a drop to drink.*

"Back to the barn," Brad picked up his train of thought. "What if we laid down plastic and set straw bales on top of it? Do you think that might hold?"

Ramone nodded. "Don't know why not."

"It would be faster than bagging. Besides, what are we going to use for sandbags?"

"I have some in my truck." Ramone motioned outside. "Kept them there just in case it flooded down at my mother's house. Since I can't get to her anyway, we can use them here."

"We could cut squares of plastic, dump sand on them, and tie them." DJ leaned against the wall of the box stall. "Or we could make tubes and tie them at both ends." She thought of all the presents she had wrapped both ways.

"Okay. You try feeding the foal again, and Ramone and I'll get started."

The phone beeped, and Brad answered it. "Sorry, Jackie, it looks like we're stuck here. No, we're safe, but there's a chance it could get wet in the barn. I know, I never thought it could happen, either, but the water's already within a couple of feet of the pump house. No, coming home won't help—you couldn't get here even if you tried. At least I know you're safer where you are." He hung up and looked at DJ.

"Deej, how about filling every container you can find with water while we have it? I wish we'd brought the stock tank up from the lower field. Hindsight is always wonderful, of course."

"Sure. Do you want me to go up to the house and fill the tubs? That's what we do at home."

"Yes, and there are some plastic jugs in the pantry. Put drinking water in those."

DJ stepped outside. Sure enough, their island had shrunk. Now water covered the long drive out to the county road. She ran up the rise to the house to do as her father had asked.

Without power for heat, the house already felt cold and damp. She turned on the water in the two tubs, filled the jugs, and pulled out all the kettles to fill, too. In spite of her father's reassuring words, she felt like a rock had taken up residence in her stomach. While the floodwater wasn't moving fast, its steady lapping up the rise reminded her that they had no control over the river.

On her way back down to the barn, she looked up at the sky, drizzling now instead of a downpour. "God, please stop the storm. I know you can do it. Please." She put buckets under every spigot and turned them on, hauling the water to the tubs she found for the arena. With everything full, she returned to the barn.

Back inside, an occasional hoof thudded against a wall and nervous nickers rippled from stall to stall as the horses let their fear be known. The sound of the river so close was very different from what they were used to.

DJ heated the bottle for the foal in the microwave and took deep breaths to calm herself. She knew panic never helped anyone, but knowing and doing were two separate things. This was like getting ready to go in the show-ring, only worse.

The filly lay sleeping.

"Ah, little one, please don't sleep your life away." DJ entered the stall, petting and talking to the mare first before approaching the foal. Head up, the foal watched her with wide, dark eyes.

"Come on, you've got to get used to me. Surely we can be friends by now." Were the filly's eyes brighter? Perkier? Or was it wishful thinking?

DJ shook her head at the thoughts that careened through her mind and knelt by the foal. "Do you want me to squirt this in your mouth or what?" Her singsong monologue at least worked to calm the mare. The filly thrashed around, trying to get her feet under her so she could run. DJ sat without moving until the baby's panic let up.

"Now that you have that over with, let's try some of this good stuff." She tickled the filly's lips with the nipple, but the foal turned her head away. "I know you should be standing to nurse from your mother, but that doesn't seem possible right now."

The mare nudged her foal and whickered deep in her

throat. "See, mind your mother, you silly thing. Either get up and get going or drink to become strong enough to get up and get going."

DJ even tried prying open the foal's jaws and forcing in the nipple, but the baby's thrashing made the mare nervous. "I wonder if we could make a sling to hold you up." DJ wet the nipple with the mare's milk again.

"Give it up for now, DJ." Brad appeared at the door. "We need your help with sandbagging."

"The pump's shot." Ramone, soaked to his waist, entered at a run.

"Get some dry clothes on, man, so you don't catch your death. We'll be filling more bags."

The horses corralled in the arena stayed in a group at the far end as they shoveled sand up from the arena floor, rolled the tubes, and tied the ends. Ramone pushed the full wheelbarrow out to the barn doors and slung the bags in place. Brad and DJ tried desperately to keep up with the filling.

After an hour, DJ's arms and shoulders felt six inches longer—and all six inches ached.

Still the water level kept rising.

They scooped, tied, and hauled faster. The helicopter flew over again, the loud voice of an emergency relief worker asking if they wanted help getting out. As before, Brad turned down the offer.

Water crept into the arena, turning the sand to mud. The horses now galloped from one end to the other, whinnying their fear.

One by one, water seeped into the stalls under the doors that hadn't been bagged or set with straw bales. However, the front and rear doors stayed dry, thanks to the bags already in place.

The team worked on, bagging and hauling, sweat running down their faces, their muscles screaming for relief.

Once all the doors had a double layer of bags in place, they stopped. Dark came early and, with it, an increase in rainfall. Ramone swept out what water had seeped in and threw down fresh straw to replace that which was soaked in the stalls.

Meanwhile, DJ and Brad hung slings of hay from the arena walls and refilled the tubs of water. As the buckets emptied, Brad set them under the downspouts from the barn roof.

"No sense wasting what clean water God sends us." He dug his fists into his back and stretched aching muscles. DJ did the same.

Never in her life had she been so tired. Every muscle in her body had cramped at one time or another in the last hours. Her feet felt like they weighed forty pounds each, and her hands hung heavy by her sides. *Good thing they're attached,* she thought, trying to lift them to take her wet gloves off.

"Come on, let's go make some dinner. There's nothing more to be done right now." Brad led the way out to Ramone's pickup truck, splashing through the water that sheeted the concrete pad. The radio spilled out flood information on the way to the house.

"The Santa Rosa area should get some relief by midnight tonight as the river crests at an anticipated twenty-five feet above flood stage. The actual crest will depend on the rainfall we receive in the next hours."

"Twenty-five feet! Last I heard we were at twenty-two. Three more feet." Brad thumped the steering wheel with the heel of his hand.

"We have to get the horses out of the barn." Ramone slumped against the door, looking as exhausted as DJ felt.

"If we let them loose, they'll all come toward the house. There's no way the water will go that high."

"What about the foal?" DJ asked.

Brad thought a moment while parking. "We'll move the mare and foal into the garage—the other one, too. With our luck, she'll drop her foal tonight." They climbed from the truck and hobbled wearily toward the door.

Brad turned on the battery-powered lamps he had set out in the kitchen. "Good thing we have a gas stove. DJ, dig under that counter, will you? The old coffeepot should be under there somewhere."

While she was searching, Brad hunted in the freezer section of the refrigerator. "I know Jackie left us some frozen soups. We better use as much frozen food as we can in case the power is off for a couple of days." He handed Ramone the sandwich fixings and took the plastic pouches of soup to the stove. Plopping them into a pan of water, he turned on the heat.

Before long, they sat down to vegetable soup and ham-and-cheese sandwiches. DJ even drank a cup of coffee well laced with hot chocolate mix.

They ate without talking, as if they hadn't seen food in a week. "Just put your things in the sink," Brad instructed. "Ramone, we'll haul up straw first for DJ to put out in the garage while you and I bring up some of those aluminum fence panels. All those mares need to do is bang into some of the stuff on the shelves and they'll go right through the roof."

He hesitated a moment. "On second thought, Ramone, you get the straw while DJ and I move the stuff from the garage into the house. That'll give us more space. We'll worry about the fence panels once that's done."

DJ felt herself sinking down into the chair. Her head jerked, and she blinked. *No time to sleep now*. She picked up her dishes and carried them to the sink. Amazing—she'd never fallen asleep that fast in her entire life.

Ramone dumped off the bales of straw and went to pick up the panels while Brad and DJ moved storage boxes,

Christmas decorations, gardening supplies, and other stuff into the house, stacking it down the hall and in the living room. She drove the lawnmower out, and Brad backed out Jackie's car.

"Okay, let's put the panels up here." He indicated the separation between the garage doors. "That way the mares will each have an entire bay." While the men fastened the fence panels, DJ spread the straw good and deep.

Back down in the barn twenty minutes later, Brad brought out blankets for each of the mares and one for the foal. "DJ, if you lead Soda, I'll carry the foal. Ramone, you bring Hannah."

They buckled the blankets around the mares and added leads with chains to loop over their noses. "Just in case we need more control," Brad said, noticing DJ's reluctance.

"Now, let's get this little one on her feet so I can pick her up."

DJ held the mare while Ramone got the baby into an almost standing position so Brad could slip one arm around her rump and another around her chest. For some reason, the filly stopped struggling, and they started the long parade up to the house. Halfway there, Brad paused to catch his breath.

"You want to trade?" Ramone asked.

Brad shook his head. "I'll make it. Let's not take a chance."

DJ lead Soda into one section of the garage and loosened the lead so the mare could investigate the surroundings. She checked on her baby first, then nosed at the aluminum panels. She took a place right beside the foal, standing guard in the strange place. With Hannah moving around in the other pen, Soda kept her body between the foal and the other horse.

"You watch them, and we'll start hauling hay. We need to get enough up here to feed everyone for at least a couple of days." Brad climbed back in the truck and waved at DJ as he and Ramone returned to the barn.

DJ shivered in the wind that blew in the open garage doors. If she was cold, what about the foal?

With bales of hay and straw stacked outside the aluminum panels to provide insulation and inside the garage to keep dry, Brad and Ramone held the mares while DJ punched the button to close the garage doors. Soda rolled her eyes at the sound of the motor and the sight of the lowering doors, but Brad kept her calm with a firm hand and his soothing voice.

"Why don't you warm the bottle up in a pan of water on the stove, DJ? If the filly won't drink it this time, we're going to have to tube-feed her again. I hate to have to do that in case something goes wrong."

"How about if I bring up some more panels and we fence off the front of the house so we can let the other horses loose?" Ramone suggested.

"Sounds like a good idea. I'd hate for all of Jackie's shrubs and flowers to get eaten and trampled, but it's a small price to pay compared to losing any horses. With the panels, we can have it both ways."

DJ took the bottle into the kitchen and set it to warm in a pan full of water. Her eyes felt so full of sand, she could barely see the numbers on the dial.

The gas lit with a bit of a pop, and she held her hands to the heat. She'd never known the meaning of bone weary before now. She had blisters on her hands from shoveling, and her muscles felt like liquid.

Never had the thought of a soak in a hot tub of water been so appealing. But getting food in that foal was far more important right now. DJ shook herself awake and tested the milk by dribbling some on her skin. Back to the battle.

With the doors closed, the garage had warmed some. She heard the truck drive back up the hill, then the sound of metal posts being driven into the ground. With each *ka-thunk* of the heavy iron sleeve that slammed down on the top of the post, she saw the mare flinch. It felt as if they were driving the posts right into DJ's skull.

And no matter what she tried, the foal refused to drink.

DJ sank down by the battery-powered lamp in the corner of the stall. "God, what can I do? This baby is getting weaker, and she could get really sick with all the weather problems we've been having. Please, please help me. Help us. Thanks for your protection from the flooding. We'd sure be grateful if you ended the storm now." She rested her head on her knees, her arms wrapped around her legs.

Soda came over and nosed DJ's hair, then whuffled and nudged her baby. The foal managed to get up on her brisket with her legs tucked under her.

"Come on, baby, all the way."

The pounding outside stopped.

DJ heard no more.

"DJ. Darla Jean."

"Huh?"

"You better get to bed." Brad knelt in front of his daughter.

"I . . . I can't. Got to feed the foal." She blinked her eyes and yawned wide enough to crack her jaw.

"Ramone and I will tube-feed her."

"No, let's try holding her up in a sling first. You guys hold her, and I'll see if I can't get her to nurse on her mother. She's gotten used to us handling her, so maybe she won't fight this time."

"I think you need to go to bed."

"Please, Dad."

At the look on his face, DJ realized what she had said. Where had the "Dad" come from? Was that really what she wanted to call him? It must be since it had just come out.

"Please."

"All right. One more try."

DJ struggled to her feet. "How are the rest of the horses?"

"Fine. We threw out hay, so they aren't exploring much right now. The generator at the barn drowned out. If I'd had time, I'd have brought it up to the house. I still might." He rubbed his forehead and his face. "Only so much you can do, I guess."

"I'll get a sheet to use for a sling, okay?"

"Yeah, fine. Ramone, come help us in here, will you?" When there was no answer, he stuck his head out the side door and called again.

Now what? DJ wondered as she took a flashlight to go in search of a sheet for a sling. *Please, there can't be one more thing to go wrong.*

15

RAMONE—WHERE IS RAMONE?

DJ tried not to think about the missing Ramone as she dug in the linen closet for an old sheet. Nothing looked remotely old in the beam of the flashlight. She finally found a stack of plain, white flat sheets down on the bottom shelf. Taking two for good measure, she headed back to the garage. Only the horses were there.

Setting the sheets on a stack of straw bales, she stepped outside, her flashlight in hand. "Brad?" The sound of her voice sent horses trotting away. They were more spooked than she was. And at this point, that was saying something. DJ shivered. "Dad?" She raised her voice.

More snorts, followed by the sound of hooves *schlupping* away.

What could have happened to them?

DJ walked toward the truck, which was parked off to the side to keep the drive clear. Both men were sitting inside. She breathed a sigh of relief. But why hadn't they answered her?

The truck was running—the drone of the idling engine told her that. Feeling as if she'd learned she was the only human left alive on the planet, DJ forced herself to go toward the vehicle.

Hand trembling, she opened the door.

Rumbling snores nearly drowned out the drone of the engine. They were both sound asleep!

DJ nibbled on her lip. Between the foaling and the flood, the two had gone for nearly two days without sleep. Should she let them sleep? But the filly needed feeding.

"Dad?" Calling him that was getting easier.

DJ waited and noticed something felt different. She looked up, and her face stayed dry. It wasn't raining!

"Dad, it quit raining!" She touched his shoulder.

He jerked as though she'd poked him with a cattle prod set on full force.

"Wha-what is it?" He peered at her, eyes owl round and blinking. "DJ, are you all right? Wha-what happened?"

"You fell asleep."

Brad let his head fall against the back of the seat. "I came to find Ramone, and he was asleep. So I thought I'd just sit in the warm cab for a minute or two before I woke him up." He scrubbed his face with both hands. "We need to feed the foal."

"Yes, we do, but guess what else is up?"

He looked at her as if answering would take too much effort.

"It quit raining!"

"Thank you, heavenly Father."

Brad's heartfelt praise brought him out of the truck, hands raised palm up.

DJ wasn't sure whether he was praising God or testing for rain, but his next words clued her in.

"No more rain. Thank you, God!"

She guessed it was both.

At his shout, Ramone jerked upright. "What's happening?"

Brad pointed toward the sky.

Ramone climbed stiffly from the truck. "How long have

I been asleep? I didn't mean to do that—fall asleep, I mean."

"No problem, Ramone. Look!" Brad pointed upward again.

"The rain stopped! Look, there's even a star up there. I was beginning to think they had all disappeared forever." Ramone thumped a hand on the hood of the truck, the noise spooking the curious horses that had gathered around them.

"Well, that's one of many major prayers answered. Now, how about the foal?"

Brad turned to Ramone. "DJ thinks we should try a sling. It might make sense now that the filly has been handled so much. If Soda will cooperate, too. . . ."

"Whatever. I'm game."

The three entered the garage, and DJ picked up the sheets. "I hope these are okay to use."

"Deej, honey, anything is okay to use at this point. Everything but us and the horses are replaceable." He took the sheets. "And you and Ramone are more important than thousands of horses—hands down."

The glow around DJ's heart radiated clear to her fingertips.

The men stroked Soda first, then approached the filly. She raised her head and appeared to be studying them. But when she didn't thrash her legs, DJ began to wonder if she was too weak to fight.

They folded the sheet the long way and slid it under the foal's belly. On three, they gently hoisted her into the air, letting her feet touch the ground. The foal scrambled for a moment but quieted again. Head up, she looked toward her mother.

"Oh, wow." DJ led Soda over to the trio. "Come on, old girl, let's make this count." *Please, God, please,* marched through her mind as DJ guided the filly toward her mother's udder.

"Please, God, let this work," she heard Brad murmur behind her.

DJ stroked the filly's head, crouching down so she could see what she was doing.

The filly started to pull away, bobbing her head and bumping the mare's flank.

"Easy, now, little one, you can do this." *Please.*

"If you can, Deej, squirt a little milk on her muzzle."

DJ aimed a teat toward the filly and squeezed. She missed.

The men moved the filly an inch or two closer.

Bump, nudge, bump. DJ pulled another stream of milk from the mare. It hit the baby's muzzle and dripped down over her lips. A pink tongue peeked out and licked the milk.

DJ held her breath.

One more bump, and the filly found the teat. She wrapped her tongue around it, pulling it into her mouth.

She began to nurse.

DJ swabbed away the tears. "She's doing it," she whispered around a throat so tight, she could hardly swallow.

"I know," Brad's voice came, reverent as a prayer. "Thank you, Father, for big favors."

"Amen to that." Ramone's voice resounded with the same awe as Brad's and DJ's.

When the foal dropped her head a good time later, the men lowered her to the straw. She sighed and lay flat out on her side.

"You earned a good rest, little one. Sleep well." Brad got up from his knees. "And speaking of sleep, I vote we all do that. Ramone, I'll pull the Murphy bed in the rec room down for you. Sorry I can't offer anyone a hot shower, but warm covers will have to do."

They trooped into the house, jerking off their boots at

the bootjack by the back door. DJ moved woodenly to her room, where she stripped off her filthy clothes with her eyes already half shut. She struggled into her sweats and, sitting on the side of the bed, pulled heavy socks over her freezing feet. She hung her head and sat there, as if frozen.

"Deej, getting into the bed before going to sleep would have been a good idea."

She felt her father lift her legs and swing them up on the bed. She tried to say thank you when he pulled the covers over her, but the effort was too great.

When she woke, weak sunlight cast a square on the hardwood floor. "The filly! She should have been fed again long ago." DJ threw back the covers and leaped into her clothes, hitting the floor running. Without waiting to put on her boots, she opened the door to the garage.

The filly stood at her mother's side, head up and under the flank, nursing on her own, her brush of a tail flicking from side to side.

DJ glanced at her watch. Nearly noon—she'd slept for hours. "Why didn't they wake me?" she muttered as she shoved her feet into her boots and pulled them on. Snagging a jacket off the peg, she stepped outside.

The clouds looked like old dishcloths, tightly wrung and tattered. But the sun managed to find the holes between them and beam its warmth down onto the soaked earth. Horses nickered, and a pair of crows flew overhead, their caws sounding more like a song of rejoicing than a threat of doom.

A line of broken sticks and grasses lay in a mud coat that showed the highest reach of the flooded river. Now the water lapped a good foot below that mark.

DJ looked down to the barns. Water still stood well up

the walls, the gray mud line above showing how far the water had already receded.

DJ drew in a deep breath of fresh air—and wished she hadn't. After working on the cleanup last weekend, she knew the smell would only get worse. Small breaths would serve her better until her nose decided to ignore the stink.

"So, everyone, where's my dad?"

"Right behind you." Brad draped an arm around her shoulders. "I'd still be sleeping if the phone hadn't rang. Your mother called to see how we are. All in all, I think she is handling this fairly well. When I said you were still sleeping, she said for you to call her back. Then I found your room empty."

"I should have called her before I went to bed."

"At 3:00 A.M.?"

"Was that what time it was?"

"Mm-hmm." Brad stretched his arms above his head and yawned. His arm thumped back on her shoulders.

"Did you see the foal nursing?"

"Yup. I checked on them around six, and she was up then."

"You coulda told me."

"What? And wake the sleeping beauty? Even I've got more sense than that."

She dug an elbow into his ribs, but not too hard.

They heard a click and a buzz behind them. The spotlight between the garage doors went on.

"Power, we've got power!" Brad spun her in a circle, then wrapped her in a bear hug. "Come on, daughter, we're going to have a *real* breakfast."

Ramone came to the door. "You have a phone call, boss."

"Thanks. How about you and DJ feed and water the horses while I make breakfast?"

Ramone nodded to where a couple of the loose horses

were drinking from the dirty floodwater. "You told them that plan yet?"

"Well, at least water the two mares from the water in the bathtubs."

The other foal was born late that Saturday night. Once again, Brad woke DJ in time. An hour later, he said, "This is what a normal foaling is like—the mare does all the work, and I cheer her on."

DJ looked over to where both Soda and her baby lay sleeping. "I'll take this kind of delivery any day. But that baby over there sure stole a piece of my heart."

"Yeah, I know. I kind of think she should be yours." At the look on her face, he put up his hands. "You earned her, you know. I might have ended up putting her down just because I didn't have time for her with all the other stuff going on."

"Dad!"

"Well, you never know. What do you think would be a good name for her?"

"Soda's Storm Clouds. I'd call her Stormy for short."

"Sounds like a winner to me." Brad shook his head. "I think I'm going to keep you on retainer as horse namer."

"Did . . . did you mean it about her being mine?" DJ was almost afraid to ask. Surely he'd been joking.

"Yes, I did. I mean I do. You'll be on her registration papers as the legal owner."

"Wow! That's so . . . I—it's just awesome." DJ turned and gave him a two-arm, rib-crunching hug as hard as her sore arms could squeeze. "Thank you. A gazillion times over, thank you!"

"Once is enough. If you squeeze my aching ribs again, I'll have to scream. And I doubt it's cool for a father to scream because of his daughter's hugs."

DJ grinned and leaned into the warmth of his side.

16

"I'M REALLY GLAD YOU'RE HOME . . . and safe."

"Me too." DJ looked up from her history book. "Come on in, Mom. I'm almost done."

Lindy sat down on the edge of the bed. "It felt like you were gone forever. And listening to the news about the water rising . . . DJ, all I could do was pray."

DJ leaned back in her chair and crossed one ankle over her other knee. "You were praying for me?"

"Yes, almost continually. As were Gran and Joe and Amy and Robert and Bobby and Billy—"

"God answered, right?"

Lindy nodded. "I've decided something."

DJ caught her breath. *Now what?* But her mother's face didn't wear gloom and doom. "What?"

"I've decided I'm going to make prayer a regular part of my life. I know Mom says we aren't supposed to bargain with God, but I told Him that if He would bring you safely home, I would put Him at the center of my life."

DJ felt like fireworks had just exploded, sending sparkles cascading in her mind.

"Now, I'm not exactly sure what I agreed to, but I intend to live up to it."

"Gran and I've been praying for you about this for a

long time." The words tumbled out. DJ knew if she said much more, she would either explode and bounce off the walls or fall apart in tears. "Have you told Robert?"

Lindy nodded. "And my mother."

"So you believe Jesus is God's son?"

"I've believed that since I was a teenager but . . ."

DJ waited for the rest of the sentence. When none came, she leaned forward. "But?"

"But I let life take over and thought I could handle it all myself." Lindy shook her head. "Silly, huh?"

DJ got up and crossed to the bed, sitting down beside her mother. "Mom, this is the best present you could ever give me."

Lindy looked up, one side of her mouth quirked in a mini smile. "Even better than an Arabian filly of your own?"

DJ scrunched her eyes as if she was trying hard to make up her mind. "Yup, even better than Stormy." Her grin said she was teasing.

With a gentle and loving hand, Lindy smoothed a lock of hair back from DJ's cheek. "Brad was so proud of you—said he couldn't have made it through without your help. I am, too. I know what a level-headed, responsible kid you are."

"Most of the time," DJ joked.

"Most of the time, yes—and what more can a parent ask for?" She hugged her daughter close. "Guess what?" she whispered in DJ's ear. "Six more days till the wedding! I think I'm going to have a nervous breakdown."

"Not with your level-headed, responsible daughter on your tail, you won't."

The two laughed and hugged again.

"If what they say about a bad dress rehearsal being good for the actual performance holds true, then this wedding will go like a dream," Lindy said when DJ came down the stairs on Saturday morning.

"Last night wasn't *that* bad." DJ smiled at her mother, sitting in Gran's wing chair with her Bible on her lap. "You look good like that."

"Like what?"

"Reading like Gran in her chair."

Lindy nodded. "It just feels right to sit here to read my Bible. Must be all those prayers that were offered up from this very place."

DJ came over and sat beside her mother's feet, leaning against Lindy's knee. "It feels good, too."

Lindy stroked down the entire length of her daughter's hair. "You have such beautiful hair, DJ. How about if I style it for you for the wedding?"

"Okay by me. Are you going to have your hair done?"

"No, Robert asked me to wear it like I always do, so that's what I'm doing. I want this wedding to be a celebration that everyone will enjoy, not a fancy show."

Three hours later, all dressed in their wedding finery, Gran, Lindy, and DJ waited in the narthex of the church. All the guests had been seated, and the organ played a medley of hymns.

"These shoes pinch my feet," DJ muttered for Gran's ears only. DJ smoothed a hand down the front of her high-necked dusty rose satin dress. The sleeves, puffed at the top and fitted from elbow to wrist, made her feel like she had stepped out of the pages of an earlier time. The toe-length skirt swished, playing a melody of its own with every move she made. If princesses felt like this, DJ figured she could handle the role. She sniffed the miniature roses and carnations in her nosegay. They smelled almost but not quite as good as a horse.

"You look lovely, darlin'. You can take the shoes off after it's over. I brought your white sandals just in case," Gran whispered back.

"Leave it to you to be prepared." DJ turned to her mother. "Mom, you look fantabulous. Are you as happy as you look?"

Lindy nodded. "You know those butterflies you talk about before a show class?" DJ nodded. "How do you get them to fly in formation?"

DJ chuckled. "I concentrate on my horse until I enter the ring. Once I'm there, they fly together like they're supposed to. Works every time."

"Okay." Lindy took a deep breath and let it all out. "Here we go. Let's enter the ring!"

At a signal from the usher, the organist began the "Wedding March," and the doors swung open.

DJ listened for the beat and started out on her left foot like she'd been told. She held her bouquet of red carnations and white lilies in front of her and rubbed the ring she wore on her thumb. The ring that Lindy would place on Robert's finger.

She glided down the aisle, smiling at Brad and Jackie in one row, and the Yamamoto family in another. Amy gave her a thumbs-up signal.

When DJ reached the front, she smiled up at Robert; at Joe, who was best man; then down at Bobby and Billy. She winked at them, and they clapped their hands over their mouths to keep from giggling.

DJ turned and watched Gran and Lindy start through the door. While the shoulder-length veil hid her mother's face, she seemed to be lit from within with a glow that turned the simple cream-colored satin dress to radiant shimmers. Beside her, Gran beamed at everyone as their march down the aisle began. Everyone stood in honor of the bride.

DJ felt like cheering and crying all at once. She wanted to jump and shout, "Hey, that beautiful woman in satin is my mother—and the other one is my grandmother."

When the completed party was at the front, DJ moved to stand beside her mother and Gran so the three of them faced the altar. The minister asked, "Who gives this woman to this man?"

Gran and DJ replied together, "We do."

"Us too," the twins added with serious faces.

DJ, Lindy, and Gran hugged each other, barely able to keep from laughing. Then Robert gently took Lindy's hand and brought her forward. DJ took her place next to her mother, and Gran moved in next to her.

Feeling someone tug on her skirt, DJ looked down into the smiling faces of the twins, one on each side.

"Are you our sister yet?" Billy—or was it Bobby?—asked in his idea of a whisper. Those at the back of the church could hear it as well as those chuckling in the front.

DJ shook her head. "Soon."

The verses were read, the soloist sang, and the vows given in strong voices.

"Is she our mother yet?" Another dual whisper.

"Soon." DJ pulled the ring off her thumb and handed it to her mother. At least her part of the ceremony was done. The rings were exchanged and prayers said. As Robert kissed his bride, Bobby and Billy grinned at each other, clapped their hands, and threw themselves at Lindy's skirts. "Now we's a family!"

Laughter rippled through the room, and Robert and Lindy hugged both the boys and DJ.

"They're right, you know," Robert said for all the guests to hear. "We *are* a family now, praise God." To the applause of their family and friends, he tucked Lindy's hand in his arm and said, "Follow us, kids." The five of them, trailed by a laughing Gran and Joe, marched back down the aisle.

"Can we eat now?" one of the boys asked.

"I want cake," stated the other.

"Soon," DJ answered again. "Very soon."

They stepped out into the bright sun, and DJ raised her face to the warm rays. The storm clouds had passed, and they were headed into a bright new day—as a family.

Coming Spring 1998!

It's all catching up to DJ Randall—her growing responsibilities at the Academy, the ongoing art projects, the piles of schoolwork—not to mention the ups-and downs of breaking in a new family. While she's happy for her mother and Robert, DJ feels more than a little jealous of her twin stepbrothers, the Double Bs, who take up more of her mother's time than she ever imagined. Does anyone have time left for DJ? And when a horse show comes in the way of DJ's art, a full-scale family war threatens to break out! Find out what happens in book #6 of HIGH HURDLES.